Some Rivers End

On the Day of the Dead

by

Eileen Clemens Granfors

D1738953

Dedication

To my teachers, all of them,

and to my friend, Denise Contreras Harder,

who dared to dream with me.

Foreword

On a spring day of our senior year, my friend Denise Contreras and I burst into our high school counselor's office, each of us proudly carrying our letter of admission to college. He looked the papers over and said, "Why bother? You're better off at junior college first."

We turned away in disbelief. Wasn't his job to counsel and encourage us?

Denise went on to graduate from San Diego State, spending her working career inspiring children in classrooms from grades kindergarten through high school. She finished her career as the principal of Palomar High School in Chula Vista, California.

I chose UCLA, despite the protests of my parents and my high school counselor. This was one of my life's best decisions, to seek a future in the great big world. I am proud to be a Bruin. After graduation, I too entered teaching, first at the junior high and then at the high school level, taking on English classes from remedial reading to AP Literature for more than three decades.

After retirement, I joined the UCLA Extension Writers' Program, making it possible for me to test another dream, one you now hold in your hands.

Eileen Clemens Granfors, September, 2010

This is a book of fiction. Any resemblance to people living or dead, places, and actions in history should be considereds purely coincidental. Any mistakes lost in translation are mine alone. Marisol, like many other Hispanic-American children, faces a world every day in which her traditions, language, culture, and future, are dependent on the whims of the winds. To all the Marisols that I have known from my childhood and teen years in Imperial Beach, California and Chula Vista, California, as well as those whom I taught, may you find books to grow on; teachers to guide and respect you; and friends who love you for who you are.

Table of Contents

Chapter 1: Ashes

The first time I saw my home in America, I said to Uncle Tomaso, "Wait, what?" People probably think it was a big house with a swimming pool and five bathrooms that amazed me, right? I wish.

He led Mama and me off the bike path through thorn bushes to sleeping bags under an oak tree. Everything smelled dusty and dry. He laughed with his fake-gold front tooth glinting, "Marisol, *mi casa es tu casa*." That was in August.

It's the beginning of October now, and I should be starting my waltzing lessons with my birthday gift certificate for eight months of dancing with Papa before my grand *quinceañera* next May.

Instead, I am living in a river camp. I am no longer new here or so creeped out about how and where we live. This river has no water. That was a first lesson about Los Angeles. Papa had told me his story again when I turned fourteen that there is a river in all of us. Did he know about this river that has no water? He knew everything. He was thinking of some kind of river in the brain or in the body. Maybe the river is part of the soul and that's why some days I still feel Papa's arms around me reading a book together. Maybe Papa's river was made of words?

I wish I could find another river, not this one because this dry river where we camp is not such a good place. We hide our lives behind the tumbleweeds that are taller than me (154.9 centimeters) and so overgrown together that our paths between them are narrow. Tomaso said the city usually cuts the tumbleweeds in the summer because of fire dangers, but they didn't do that this year (budget cuts). It's also why we can't have a campfire or a stove in camp. He says it's better for us that the city ignores the river valley.

Some Rivers End on the Day of the Dead

Each group has their own camp under their own oak tree. The best, tallest, widest oak trees are the furthest from the houses across the street. We didn't get one of those trees. There are twelve or fourteen camps at this end of the river valley, with most camps for working men like my uncle Tomaso. A few of the men have women with them and sometimes I hear women's laughter on pay day nights, but I haven't seen any children because the women work during the day too so they leave their children with their *abuela* probably in Mexico as we left my baby brothers, Diego and Hermes.

The tumbleweeds scratch my skin, leaving itchy spots, and the dust is always up my nose making me sneeze. Our oak tree is short, but we use the branches to put up blankets for some privacy. We have dug a hole under the oak tree to keep our valuables in a coffee can, our passports and savings money. The river valley is wider than the football field at school. Power towers rise in the middle of it maybe fifty meters apart. I would convert that to yards if I were better in math, like my friend at home, Natividad, who is practically a mathematical genius.

It is hard enough to be fourteen, still a child in the eyes of the family, beginning to grow up in the eyes of the boys at school. Since school started, I have studied the boys at my school when we are doing silent reading or running around the track. None of them have the dark good looks of the dangerous boys like Puma at home or even Tomaso, and certainly none matches up to my father, who was tall and dark like Antonio Banderas or Helio Castaneves. I want to be fifteen and celebrate my *quinceañera* and know my place and maybe find the river in me that is not this dry, ugly river. The river in me would be fresh and clear and open to the sea.

I don't always like my time at school where the rich kids drive away in their cars at lunch time and some of us stand in line for a free lunch that tastes like paste no matter what the hair-net ladies think they are serving us. School lunch was a second lesson about Los Angeles. I eat the fruit because fruit can't be ruined by the mixer machine. Mama works hard as a nanny, but we can't pay an apartment deposit. I wish other kids my age lived here in the arroyo so I had someone to talk to; then again, I wouldn't wish this kind of life on anyone who is my friend. I miss Paloma's laughing and Natividad's wise cracks and the way time passed so fast at school or at home when we were together.

When I go to school each day, I tell myself, at least I am clean and I smell good. Why do the rich kids wear torn uniforms that they call hot, and some of them even let their hair stink and that's cool? If one of the poor kids stinks, kids text each other and laugh behind their hands.

I remember back to the first week of school, and I will retell it exactly as it happened to me:

The teacher said something rude and stupid. I stay after class to talk to her. Until this moment, I liked her best. Still, my father taught me not to assume, but to ask, because if you assume, it makes "an ass of *u* and me." He learned that saying in journalism school. Papa said the only exception about assuming is for family and taxes because I can always trust my family, and taxes will always go up. Every day he reminded me there is a river in all of us, and that no one can step into the same river twice. I understand that second part. Rivers change the way waves at the beach do, always new ones. But the first part, I nodded as if I understood that, thinking he must see the water go down the throat so that it comes out you know where, but now things have changed, it's too late, I cannot ask him.

I will ask this teacher about her rudeness, and Papa, I will try to tell you of all the things I do and see in America that we would have laughed about or maybe we would have investigated further to avoid assuming. He had so many words of wisdom for me, and when I didn't understand I should have asked, but he also included another rule where he said I should learn restraint, which means not blurting or butting in.

Was it because he butted in that he's dead, and we're hiding? And even so early in the school year, here I go, butting in with this teacher.

Some Rivers End on the Day of the Dead

"Marisol?" the teacher asks, and I'm shocked she knows my
name on the third day of the school year. The other teachers are
still using seating charts except for Coach Sneed, who calls all us
ninth graders one name—Bozo plus our line up number-- and the
math teacher since he doesn't use seating charts and probably won't
learn our names ever.

"Mrs. Kovacs, I don't understand why you would say we are
slow like most asses," I say. It bothers me to think she called us
stupid and slow like donkeys. Nati taught me there are Mexican
asses like burros and American asses like butts. Her father, Mr.
Cho, wanted us to quit saying asses.

"Do all American teachers say these things? Before this all
my teachers were nuns." I don't tell her my other school was in
Tijuana although Papa only spoke English to me and to my
brothers so we would grow up bilingual for when his assignment
finished and returned us to the U.S.A.

Mrs. Kovacs runs her fingers through her curly gray hair,
which is cut into layers and looks like a cabbage. She laughs and

laughs. Her nose whistles. "No, honey, not asses." She writes on the white board. "Look. They are slow as MOLASSES. That's called an idiom, an expression that doesn't translate exactly. It's like a nickname, but for language. Okay? Do you know the word *molasses?*"

I laugh too. "American idioms could cause some problems for me. I understand when I see the words, but hearing them, not so much."

"Why don't you keep a list of them? Our English class will work on lots of things, and I will add idioms to our list." She turns to jot a note on her grade book on the lectern and then picks up a hall pass paper. "I'll write you an excuse for your history class with Mr. McKee. We don't want him to think you're as slow as molasses." We both smile, I take the pass, and for the first time, I think maybe I will like ninth grade at East Valley High School in Santa Dorena. It is north of Los Angeles and far from my Mexican home.

Some Rivers End on the Day of the Dead

Life isn't fair here in America. I goofed up when I assumed it would be. This is the most surprising lesson I have learned so far, except for new idioms with Mrs. K.

.

Fire leaps far away against the sky. The wind blows and blows, throwing off the smell of burning things. On the mountaintops, the wind whips the flames into whirling plumes, but we'll be safe unless the wind changes directions, which it won't, not in the fall in Southern California.

That's what Uncle Tomaso says. He has traveled here to live and work for three years with his green card to make it legal. If it wasn't legal, he would probably do it anyway. Tomaso is not fond of obeying someone else's rules.

He also says rain is worse than fire, which I don't believe at all.

I beg Mama for the same thing each night. "Please, Mama. Let's go home. To *Abuela's*. To Tijuana."

Some Rivers End on the Day of the Dead

Her smile turns down a little. I shouldn't hurt her like this when she is trying so hard. Her hair is gray along the part between her black braids and her body is a rectangular block, like a tamale. She pats my hand the same as every night and gives me the same answer too.

"Marisol, *querida*, Marisol de Lira Lima, life is safer here. This is what your father would have wanted. It was our plan to return to America for your high school years, after your *quinceañera*. So now you and I are here sooner. You will get your education and become a famous American doctor or lawyer or business woman or whatever your heart desires." She points to the north. "Look across the street, right there. We will own a house that big some day."

I look. Because we are low in the Santa Dorena riverbed, I see only the top stories of the house and the brick wall the homeowners put up. I know the house because Mama works there, and I do my homework there and most mornings, I get ready for school in the shining bathroom. I don't want that big house. I want my old life, with my brothers and my grandmother and my two aunts.

I want Paloma and Natividad to walk to with school each day, telling secrets on the dusty street as we had since we were little ones. My old school, I guess our colors were black and white, with the nuns who pressed their lips tight as they scolded us about our short skirts (black) turned up at the waistbands or our blouses (white) pulled out. The nuns said, "*No todo lo que brilla es oro.*"

But we wanted to shine like gold. We used to sketch in our notebooks to share at recess what we would wear to school if we could. I dreamed of a mini-dress in the bright colored squares of a Mondrian print (Tia Gloria is an art major). The dress has a fringed edge that swings when I walk. So do my triple-bangled earrings. I wear poofy hair and short boots. Paloma drew baby clothes with ruffles for her someday, and Nati concentrated on the preppy look. Dress codes apply to all schools, American or Mexican. I should believe clothes aren't important since only our *calavera*, our skull and skeleton, is our real self. But that turns my thoughts to Papa.

Some Rivers End on the Day of the Dead

In my dreams, my papa is alive, his skull not broken open in the street like he was a used *piñata* for the trash after the party.

Gangster people hated my father's newspaper reporting, and for that, they shot him. The police and Papa's newspaper said this same thing, that Papa was a double agent, a double crosser, playing both sides against the middle. He was the fourteenth journalist to die in the drug wars. He had told us not to worry, that he was careful and balanced in his reporting. I am afraid this was an assumption on his part. He became a target as if his head had a set of red circles on it instead of wavy black hair and bright white teeth and his Zorro mustache, no matter what he said. Tomaso says the drug war gets worse every week now.

For that, we ran away, Mama and me, before Papa's funeral, before saying a proper goodbye or honoring him. We didn't have even Tomaso's so-called friends to help us reach the U.S. I say *so-called* friends because he fights with them almost every Saturday night over a pretty girl or who pays the bar bill or who drinks how many bottles of beer in the camp.

Some Rivers End on the Day of the Dead

We couldn't cross the border even with our American passports because some of the cops are crooked and work for the gangsters from the drug cartel. They would have found Mama and me for sure. One thing about the bad boys is that even they respect babies and grandmothers, which is lucky, because Hermes and Diego and *Abuela* would not have made our trip any easier, and I can't imagine trying to live with all of them in the river camp with us.

The bus dropped us off at the marina in Ensenada, we paid a fishing boat captain, and he took us north in choppy seas. Mama and I were both sea sick, the captain laughed and said we were chumming for him. I didn't care if he laughed or threw me overboard. I was too sick and too sad. My arms and legs felt like cement sacks the workers were using to build a fence at *Abuela's*.

The boat chugged slowly, bobbing in the waves, to a beach north of San Diego but south of Los Angeles. Our clothing packs got wet while the boat idled outside the breakers at low tide, and we jumped into the shallows. Mama had our traveling money and our passports in a plastic bag in a back pack in a trash bag. Felipe met us, took some of our money to drive us here, to Santa Dorena, where Tomaso waited.

We expected an apartment, but he showed us the river camp and said it was a better hiding place. He chewed his lip, acting as if he didn't quite believe his own words. This was in the month of August.

The first night, I crawled into the sleeping bag and cried and cried. Mama held me, but she cried too, and then she told me my favorite story about how she met my father when he was twenty and she was eighteen. She makes it sound like a fairy tale, beginning, "Once upon a time in Rosarita, . . . " I fell asleep listening, and in the morning we went to register for the American school.

We have changed our names in America. I am Marisol DeLira at school. No Lima for Papa, and when I dropped even his name, I dropped a chunk of my heart to leave back on the street with his blood and his broken skull.

Some Rivers End on the Day of the Dead

The shrub oaks jitter, and I pull my sleeping bag higher. I hear the coyotes howling, the men in the other camp laughing, their radio too loud, and they are drunk. I hope Uncle Tomaso won't bother to shush them because someone will want to fight him. He is smaller than the other men, like a bantam rooster, and he likes to fight to prove he can take it. He has no restraint. He assumes people will listen to him, even when he is drunk.

When he is not fighting, Tomaso is funny, singing about girls with pretty brown eyes and telling stories of the hundreds of girls who have fallen in love with him. Mama throws a serape over his head when he is too silly. He is Papa's younger brother. She spoils Tomaso with foods he likes and makes excuses for his behavior. He is like my papa except that he has more muscles, less sense, and his hair is jet black with no gray in it. He begins the day wearing a kerchief around his neck, but by afternoon it winds around his forehead. He says it's his trademark, like Papa's Zorro mustache. Tomaso does not have perfect teeth or even a perfect replaced front tooth since he let the dentist use a cheap alloy instead of real gold. *"No todo lo que brilla es oro,"* Papa would say just like the nuns. Everything shiny is not gold. I know this. Does Mama? Does Tomaso? Does he think his fancy tooth fools anyone that he is a rich man?

Since Papa died, Tomaso is shorter, or he walks shorter, with his shoulders stooped forward, as if he is carrying Papa's death like a burden to his soul. To me, Tomaso is immature and selfish, and I am ashamed when I wish he could be dead instead of my papa.

Noise thunders above us. A sheriff's helicopter shines a light into our arroyo, and a voice calls down, first in English and then in Spanish, "Evacuate. Go to the school." A hush falls as the copter moves farther north along the river bed. Mama and I begin to pick up the paper bags with our clothing and my schoolbooks for tomorrow. We get ready to push the purple shopping cart up the gravel path. Tomaso says "No need, no problem." He must be right since no one else is moving or packing. Are the sheriffs trying to scare us so they can deport us? Mama and I have our passports.

The wind picks up. Mama pulls me to lie down in our sleeping bag zipped together under the oak tree. Our hair gives off static electricity that makes us jump. Ashes blow towards us, falling like snow. Tomaso hands me a kerchief he has gotten wet from our five-gallon jug of fresh water. I tie the scarf over my mouth and nose. We'll stay. The three of us say our rosary with a special prayer to St. Florian.

"Sleep, ladies. I will be your St. Florian," says Uncle Tomaso. He smiles in our direction, but he looks across us to the oak tree and then up into the smoky sky. His mouth closes in a firm line.

As impossible as it seems, I sleep.

Chapter 2: Mañana

I am watching my *abuela* make tortillas. Her hands are small but fast and flashing into the dough, scoop-pat-scoop-pat-scoop-pat.

The kitchen is warm as sunbeams. Remiendos, our *gato calico*, paws at the striped curtains. *Abuela* continues, scoop-pat-scoop-pat. Remmy swings from the curtain and leaps to the floor, purring.

My chair is next to Papa's. He is reading to me from the newspaper and explaining headlines and the pictures. He shows me his name on the article about Tijuana's mayor. I am proud of him and pat his cheeks and pull his glasses off. He laughs and tries to

finish reading me his story. It's hard to concentrate when I smell
pork roasting, burning, in the pit, tortillas as they fry in the skillet,
onions in the beans de olla.

My stomach growls loudly, and I push against my belly.
Oh, I am too fat. My skirt will need to be unbuttoned for school,
and I will have to pull my sweater down over it. Paloma, who is as
round as a meatball in albondigas soup, will tell me to quit worrying
about my body shape, just like Sister Jacinta does. Sister Jacinta is
also round as a meatball.

A crow caws from the oak tree, and I open my eyes. I have
been dreaming of home. Mama has already gone to work. The
morning air is gray and smoky. The burned smell clings to my
clothes, my hair, my skin. My uncle stoops under the oak tree
where we have a small cooler, wrapping tortillas and beans for his
lunch.

He watches me shift up on my elbows in my sleeping bag.
"Get up *paraquito, poco de sol.*" He laughs, and his gapped front teeth
make him look less handsome than when his mouth is closed. "You

see, Tomaso was right. No fire reached us. Trust your Uncle Tomaso, Marisol," he says, even though he looks away when I glance into his eyes. Why does he bother to say this? Of course family is one of the two things a girl can trust.

Two makes me think of two other story endings. If Tomaso had been with us at home maybe then he could have won the fight or tried to fight and lost. Either way, Papa would not be dead. Or the other way, where they miss Papa with their gun shots and drive away and then we move here to a real house.

When Tomaso sees my crinkled forehead, he begins singing,

Marisol es el sol,

Marisol es el mar,

Marisol, Marisol, Marisol. . . .

He holds the last *Marisol* like a mariachi singer.

I wish I could return to my dream, leave this foreign life, this dirty camp, the dirty looks I get at school from the rich white kids. I want the way things used to be, the old river that lived in me. I do not want to wait for Mama's promise of someday or a big house or a long journey to a new river. I want my old home, my old

family. I want it to be last June. I want to control the future so that

the month of August doesn't even exist or it didn't happen the

same way.

Uncle Tomaso shakes the bottom of my sleeping bag,

rolling it up and up with his strong hands until I am rolled out into

the morning's cooler air. I don't want to pee in the oleander bushes

where the others do. I grab a blanket from the tree, wave at

Tomaso, and run across the street from our arroyo camp to the

house where Mama works. If Mama signals that Mrs. Beauman is

gone, I can use their bathroom to get ready for school. I like to be

clean for school.

After coming through the backyard gate, I hug the pepper

tree and squeeze my thighs tight. I peek under the lowest limb,

waiting for Mama's signal. If Mama doesn't signal soon, I will have

to pee right here, and I'll have to go to school without a shower

and spend all morning sniffing at my armpits and worrying about

being odoriferous as Mrs. K says when someone like Stan farts in class, and everybody starts waving their Peechee folders around and coughing or holding their noses. It's high school, but my classmates act like my baby brothers half the time, at least the boys do and that one girl, one of the Jens.

Mama steps onto the back porch, whipping a bath mat and holding the baby, Andy, on her hip. Andy has a blue pacifier that his mother calls a binkie in his mouth. He smiles around it and points at the trees. I run into the house that smells of air freshener and baby powder. These scents are chemical, coming out of a bottle. They make my nose itch, and I am afraid I will sneeze. What would it be like to live here? In Baja our house smells of lemons and tortillas and flowers and sugar and sweaty children, smells from nature, not sprays.

Mama hands me my clothes that she washed this morning with the baby's things, including Andy's cloth diapers because the Beaumans don't believe in Pampers. They also don't believe in doing their own laundry. The clothes smell fresh and clean even if it from chemicals instead of the wind. I step into the front bathroom.

Some Rivers End on the Day of the Dead

In the shower my stuffed sausage feeling leaves. My too-tight pants aren't on. My skin looks browner when it is wet though, and I wish it would like look like Mrs. Beauman's, which is white as rice paper. She has black hair like me, hers short and curly, and mine straight and long with bangs chopped across my forehead. Mama says after my *quinceañera*, no more bangs! Mrs. Beauman has green eyes. In her picture in the living room, she is lifting a smaller baby Andy to the sky, and she is smiling like any mother smiles at her baby. I wish Mama would tell Mrs. Beauman about me. Maybe she would help us. Maybe she wouldn't. I don't know Americans very well although I am learning the idioms by keeping a list.

I clean the bathtub with a towel, clean as a whistle (that's an idiom that makes no sense to me) and slip on my school uniform of khaki jeans and the blue school shirt the counselor gave me the day I enrolled. I wear a tank top underneath for the walk home in the hot afternoon. My jeans are hard to pull up my legs and hard to button even when I suck in my breath. I leave my t-shirt, blanket and pajama bottoms on the counter for Mama to bring home tonight along with Tomaso's clean kerchiefs. I don't know this writing, *Cincinnati* on my sleep t-shirt, but Uncle Tomaso says it is baseball from a city far away. I know stuff like that for school in case anyone talks to me. In class, the teachers are fair, except the yelling of Coach Sneed, but at nutrition and lunch, the other kids ignore me or they choose one of us to make fun of.

I open the bathroom door to be on my way. But I stop because of voices in the kitchen. This is not Mama talking to Andy. It is Mama talking to Mrs. Beauman. I look at the bathroom window. I can't fit through that little slice of light. I tip toe to the corner of the living room and the hall way, thinking I can sneak out. I hear car keys and Mrs. Beauman's voice and Andy's fussing.

"Bye bye again, little love." She makes kissing sounds. Andy's fussing turns to giggles.

"Auda?" She pronounces my mother's name the American way, A-duh instead of our soft Mexican Ow-da but it is better than at first when she hired Mama, because then Mrs. Beauman thought Mama's name was *sabroso*. Tomaso, who worked on a tree-trimming crew that day, had told her Mama's cooking was delicious, *sabroso*.

We still laugh when we eat something *muy sabroso*. We call Mama

Santa Sabrosa for a joke among us. Tomaso also says Mrs.

Beauman's green eyes make him think of something hot, like chili

verde, but she is too skinny for him, plus she's married, and even

Tomaso should know better than to flirt with a married white

woman, I hope.

"Yes?"

"Make extra flan for tonight. Tom likes it."

"Yes, Missus. *Gracias por la mole.* Don't worry. Dinner will

be *muy sabroso*." Mama is walking Mrs. Beauman to the door. With

Mrs. Beauman ahead of her, Mama rolls her eyes, asking the saints

for patience. "*Teléfono* if there's more?" Mama's voice sounds

humble, and a word that means as if she would polish Mrs.

Beauman's boots and not just her silverware and her toilets and her

baby's butt. Is the word *meek?* At home, Mama is kind, not meek.

Mrs. Beauman hesitates at the door, rubbing her neck and

rolling her shoulders. "I was thinking how wonderful it would be to be you for a day, Auda. I would stay home and hang Andy's diapers on a clothesline, no matter what the homeowners association says about no clotheslines in any yards."

I almost lose restraint and blurt a few things at her. She leaves.

Mrs. Beauman thinks a lot of crazy things--that she and Mama are so much alike because they love chocolate and baby Andy. She thinks she would like hanging laundry on a line! She should see my short *abuela* hanging clothes on a windy day.

So alike. . . I can picture this fancy lady squatting under an oleander to pee or using the city's dog waste bags to poop into. I go to school fresh and clean and smiling because already today I have proven I am a better person than I used to be.

Coach Sneed tells us to try to improve just one percent each day. Who can't do one percent? My one percent is that I have started to learn restraint. Papa would be proud except he'd remind me not to brag about myself.

Chapter 3: Rollercoaster

I get to school with my hair a mess from the wind and sweaty from the heat, going through the morning with all my least favorite classes, science, math, PE, and art. I am good in three of those subjects, but each of the teachers has different rules, like no rules in math for where you sit and I'm always trying to find a seat where I can see the SmartBoard but not too close so that I get called on a lot. In PE there's Coach Sneed with his yelling, and art where there is a good teacher but I am a hopeless artist. Are you all thumbs? Mrs. K asked me when I told her about art, and I looked at my hands and shrugged. She added "all thumbs" to our list of idioms.

Some Rivers End on the Day of the Dead

After lunch I have Mrs. K's class. She smiles when she reads to us from books, and she doesn't get mad if we call her teacher or Mrs. K. She puts up funny cartoons on the Powerpoint, and she chooses groups. Some people hate that because they want to get into a group where someone else will do all the work, but Mrs. Kovacs knows every trick in the book and so she puts all the lazy boys together in one group and watches them to see how they will manage to do the assignment since none of them read the homework. The first weeks it was the easy book *Of Mice and Men*, and I thought I was surrounded by idiots because they were not willing to read it. I feel like I share a laugh with Mrs. K on the Q.T, another idiom.

I met my friend, Sylvan, in our first groups. Mrs. Kovacs put us together to draw a map of the hurdles George and Lennie faced to try to reach their dream. The homework was to draw a map of our own hurdles, which I faked because who would believe a hurdle is making sure I have a shower each morning and that another hurdle is hiding so a drug gang can't find me, making me live under an oak tree? Who would believe that my father was

murdered for telling the truth?

On the group map we could make mountains or raging

rivers and in some places bridges where they made a plan to help

things go right for them. We read that book very fast, and I liked it

except the sad ending because the gun and George with his friend

reminded me of Papa, and I hope that in the moment he was shot,

Papa was looking at a dream of his, like of dancing with me at my

quinceañera or of my university graduation or of walking on the

beach with Diego and Hermes and me, jumping the waves and

chasing the sea gulls, a memory like one of those. Our family shares

many happy memories of my beautiful Papa.

My friend, Sylvan, is good with English words. We had two

cheerleaders in our group with us, Britney and Brittany, and they

were very smart and very nice, which was news to me about the

social groups here at East Valley High School because I had

watched all those cheerleader movies when I was twelve and

believed every cheerleader would be a phony little snot. At school the girls look sort of alike in our everyday khaki uniforms, that's the point, so the cheerleaders wear bows in their pony tails with their pony tails pulled over to the left side. Other people copy them, but the whole school knows who is a cheerleader and who isn't.

Sylvan and I walk around the track at lunch time. She is on the free lunch program too even though she is not a minority. Her name seems kind of strange for an American, but she says her grandmother is a hippy person so of course her name has to do with trees. I don't get it, but I don't tell her. I picture her grandmother with wide hips like *mi abuela*.

Sylvan says my name is the most beautiful name she ever heard. I think so too because Papa told me he chose this name. "Of all the things in the world, I love the sea and the sun," said Papa. "Your mother is the sun because she is constant, and I am the sea because I am unpredictable, and now we have you, Marisol, to be like both of us." This story makes me proud, but it also makes my heart hurt.

Some Rivers End on the Day of the Dead

I'm glad I'm not just another Jennifer. We call the three we know tall-Jen, short-Jen, and crazy-Jen. When you say it fast it's like Taljen, Shojen, and Zejen. No one has a nickname for me yet because my name is one of a kind, like me, the sun and the sea together. I wish my middle name was Rio for the river in me instead of Maria.

When Sylvan and I walk at lunch, we hardly talk at all. Actually, I hardly talk at all, and she talks a lot. It seems like Sylvan is the sister I never had, and a substitute for Paloma and Nati. I've told her things I never told other people here like I've had my period for two years. She hasn't started yet, but she keeps tampons in her backpack.

I keep secrets from her though. She doesn't know where I live. She assumes I live in the low-income apartments that are mostly old people and drug addicts. She told me about the trailer park where she lives. At lunch, we hang out and let ourselves laugh.

"Look at that," Sylvan says. Two big boys are trash-canning Stan from our English class. He's Bozo 1 in PE because his last name is Applegate. Kids call him Road Apple. He laughs like it's a good nickname.

"We should help him," I say, but then one of the biggest jock boys walks over and helps Stan.

"Marisol, no matter what my grandmother says, the two of us can't change the world. You have to be big or famous or rich, like that guy." Sylvan stops walking and changes her red backpack to her other shoulder. She is so skinny, I think the backpack weighs more than she does. Her eyes are brown and her hair is blonde except the tips that she dyed green to match her name. She's pretty even though Uncle Tomaso would tell her to eat more lard in her frijoles, especially since she says she is five feet, six inches, which I should be able to convert to metrics, but I can't.

If I could take her to my house, she could ask Mama what food to eat so that she would get her period. It's embarrassing to be in ninth grade and not have progressed to that step of womanhood yet. Mama was proud and sad at the same time when

Some Rivers End on the Day of the Dead

I told her about mine. Papa gave me a big hug and asked me how I grew up so fast. I was a little embarrassed about this with Papa.

"Do you know that guy?" Sylvan asks.

"Duh, how would I know anybody like that? I wish."

"He's Coach Sneed's son. Can you believe that?"

"No way. Coach is a jerk."

We walk some more and then we go to sit outside Mrs. Kovacs' classroom. Mrs. K eats lunch by herself, grading papers with her door opened a few inches using the door stop. Sylvan and I lean back against the cement building. Usually we sit and read. One time we helped Mrs. Kovacs so that she wouldn't feel down in the dumps when she opened her door. Someone had written "Book Bitch" in pencil across the outside of her classroom door because a book report was due. We cleaned the words off with orange soda and Sylvan's sweatshirt.

We think Mrs. Kovacs is funny even if no one else in the class laughs at her jokes. She suggests books for us to check out and if anything ever happened to Mama or Tomaso and I couldn't find my way back to *Abuela's*, I would want to live with Mrs. K

though Sylvan says that's really stupid because ICE would send me

back before I could even say Mexico. This makes me upset that

Sylvan assumes I'm illegal, like everybody else does. I've told Sylvan

I am a U.S. citizen like my father, I have my papers, the school has

my records, I was born in San Ysidro, but she says yeah right,

whatever. I had lived in Mexico for twelve years of my fourteen. I

am not only bilingual, but I have dual citizenship or maybe it's duel

citizenship because the Mexican and American parts of me are

always fighting.

Sylvan is digging around in her overstuffed backpack. "I

forgot my book. Let's go back to the locker. We have time."

I want to tell her to go by herself because I need to read the

end of the chapter in this impossible book Mrs. K reads with us but

then assigns chapters from too. It is called *Great Expectations*, and

she says that's what she has for all of us.

All I know is that it is a very great expectation for her to

think her students can read this book if she is not reading it to them. The class is begging to go back to *Of Mice and Men*, even the kids who never read anything anyway, because at least they liked to hear Mrs. K read Lennie's funny voice, "Tell me about the rabbits, George." Everybody laughed every time she read Lennie's parts.

But I go with Sylvan. She would go with me. We get to the locker, and she pulls her book out. All the pages have dog ears, and Sylvan has post-it note markers in about twenty pages because she has questions to ask. The lines in the cafeteria are shorter now that it's later, and we can go in and get a part of our lunch, an apple for me, a scoop of mac and cheese in a cup for Sylvan. Sylvan pulls her orange soda from her backpack to share with me. Even though the soda is warm now, it's better than school water fountains or the milk that's practically spoiled at the cafeteria.

As we approach, one of the marching band boys throws a pickle slice from his burger at Taljen from Mrs. K's class. Taljen's a big deal in the Drama Club. When I first came, I thought people were calling them emus, like the ostrich birds, but they are Emos.

Some Rivers End on the Day of the Dead

The Emo group screams and rockets back little pellets, the breath mints they eat instead of real food.

Soon the quad is a pandemonium of flying food and shrieking kids. The two young teachers on yard duty have been talking under the canopy with coffee cups in their hands. They look shocked as if there's an earthquake, and the pretty one with muscular arms, the cheerleader advisor, squawks into her walkie talkie.

Sylvan and I run from the lockers to watch the fun, but then I am afraid because I don't want to get into trouble. Trouble at school means suspension and no free breakfast, no free nutrition snack, no free lunch. Mama would be very angry with me if the school told her I was suspended, especially for something as stupid as wasting food.

"Marisol, come on," Sylvan pushes me in the back. "Let's get in there and have some fun!" She swings her arms around and around like a boxer getting ready for the ring. "Why are you such a wussy girl?"

"No." I look at her and she starts to grab me, but then she seems to get it.

We turn away from the quad, towards the locker room and Mrs. Kovacs' classroom, which is our safe zone. The assistant principal, Mr. Moore blows his whistle in our faces. He is paunchy although his face is narrow. He should be *Huevo Nuevo* because he's like a shiny egg with the East Valley blue staff shirt and khaki pants on.

"You two. Stop. Sit." The concrete has been hosed down. It is gooey and wet and smells like the smushed tuna sandwich the hoses missed, there are no benches, and Sylvan throws her folders down. We each sit cross-legged on them and wait.

Mr. Moore repeats this routine as he walks along until at least fifty kids are sitting wherever he has pointed. Ten kids haven't caught on or don't care and food continues to fly. Coach Sneed arrives on the run in his gym shorts and t-shirt. Some idiot tosses a banana peel at the back of his head. It sticks to his neck. Coach Sneed turns purple as he does when people are running laps like snails in track. I cannot picture a running snail, but I hate it when Coach Sneed yells that and turns purple.

Sylvan begins edging back towards the building, pulling me from behind by my belt loops. We move slowly without looking. No one will miss us if we can get to the locker room and close the door. We won't need to worry about being suspended. The other kids call suspension a joke. They sit at home while their parents work, they have liquor parties and sex parties, watch dvds all day. That's what they say. I don't know what Sylvan does at home, but I go to Mrs. Beauman's and help Mama with Andy or scrub the Beauman's toilets if we have a school holiday that is not an everybody holiday. The first one was California Admissions Day, which I thought was going to be like going to confession and saying an admission of guilt. The second one was last week for Columbus Day. In Mexico, Christopher Columbus is no hero and doesn't get a holiday. Paloma and Nati would be jealous about the extra holidays, especially Paloma who wants only to graduate and marry Alejandro.

Some Rivers End on the Day of the Dead

Since I am friends with Sylvan, it's better being at school than being away from school. We bump to a stop against the curb that surrounds the quad, and we know we're almost safe. We can close the locker hallway door and tell the teachers we were afraid of all the trouble.

Sylvan lets go of my belt loops, but leans forward and whispers in my ear. "Oh-oh."

I look over my shoulder.

Mrs. Kovacs has her hands on her hips. She is not smiling. I look out at the quad, and there are Sylvan's folders left where we should be sitting. I know about incriminating evidence because I read Agatha Christie for Mrs. Kovacs' first book report. I seem to be, as the idiom goes, in a pickle.

Chapter 4: Surprises

Mrs. Kovacs offers only a stern "Tsk Tsk," as she crooks her finger to indicate we should follow her.

Coach Sneed hollers, "Hey. Those two bozos belong here," pointing at Sylvan's folders. But Mrs. K walks right over to the folders and picks them up, pulling an office referral form from her shoulder tote bag that is stuffed with books and a million papers. She waves the pink referral paper at Coach Sneed, saying. "I'll take care of these two and the paperwork. I had my eye on them."

Sylvan's mouth is a round O, and I can't believe Mrs. K would treat us like the rest of the kids either. I thought she liked us because we like her. Mrs. K returns to us and hands Sylvan her folders and takes us by the elbow and walks us into her classroom.

Some Rivers End on the Day of the Dead

"Sit," she says, and then she begins to write on the white board with markers. "Sylvan, type this agenda into a PowerPoint for me, please." The only thing on the agenda is the word *essay*. Nobody is going to like that after such a crazy lunch. Why can't we have a discussion?

"What about the office?" Sylvan asks, and I want to slug her because maybe Mrs. K forgot.

"What office?" she answers and rips the referrals. She tosses them into the trash can. "Mr. Sneed won't remember. Let's not let the cat out of the bag, okay? You know that one, right, Marisol?

"Yes, Mrs. K." And I think of the day Mrs. K taught us that expression after I asked a question about George and Lennie before we watched the film and before we talked about it, and how the other kids complained that I was providing TMI. Stan said beaners always ruin everything, but Mrs. K didn't hear him, and I didn't tell. Then when Mrs. K showed the film everybody was acting like total dorks.

Some Rivers End on the Day of the Dead

The class broke into cheers at the ending of the film, even though I had tears on my face. They were laughing and pushing and pretending to shoot one another in the head as the bell rang, and I stayed in my seat pretending to look in my backpack. Mrs. K found her tissue box and asked if I was getting a cold even though I assume she knew I was crying about the film.

"Bring your thinking caps tomorrow," she had told us, and Barry high-fived Stan, knowing they would get to break rule Number 3c of the dress code.

The next day Sylvan lingered by Mrs. K's desk, rummaging through her backpack.

"Mrs. K?"

"What's up?"

"*Mice and Men* is the first book I ever read the whole thing of." She pulled her knotted shirt down to cover her midriff.

"Did you like the book?"

"I liked it until the end. I liked that Lennie. I liked George for caring about Lennie. Why'd Steinbeck end the book that way? Shit. . . I mean, dang, I didn't like it when they shot the dog either."

"That's why you're wearing your thinking cap tomorrow. I want you to think about why Carlson killed Candy's dog and why George acted as he did and think about how you feel about it. We'll have a group discussion and get everybody's opinion."

"But those fools make it a big joke." She angled her head, indicating the mobs slamming locker doors.

As it turned out, Sylvan was right. Of course, our classmates made the exercise into a circus. We spent ten minutes trading hats and ten minutes talking about bed-head hair and maybe ten minutes talking about George and Lennie though a lot of the class, led by Stan, wanted to talk about Curly's wife because they like to call her a tramp and a 'ho.

"Books aren't just some big joke are they for you two?" Mrs. K's question brings me back to the present. We look around the classroom, shelves filled with books, book covers on the bulletin boards, book lists for the taking stacked by the books to check out from the book rack. Zejen twirls the book rack until it falls over or the books fly off.

"I want to be a pediatrician or a vet," Sylvan says. "Do you have any books about doctors or animals?" She stops for a second. "Or poor people?"

"Whichever book you want, go ahead and take it home for as long as you want."

"Nah, my Granny Linda, she volunteered to rent the movie so I could pass my book report on *The Andromeda Strain,* but then I read most of it, and she did too. She wants me to focus on science, so I can save the environment, not reading a fiction book." Mrs. K walks along the front of the classroom, touching the books on the marker pen tray.

"Is this book about an astronaut? My granny. . .she's okay with books about our futures." Sylvan is holding *Stargirl*.

"I think you'd like that book. It's one of my favorites. It's about an original thinker and peer pressure." She picks up *Jane Eyre*.

"Here's another one to look over. See which one you like better. If your Granny asks about it, tell her it's extra credit. Most parents out here will do anything for extra credit."

"That's cool." Sylvan stuffs the books into the bottom of her backpack.

"You're going to make a very good doctor, Sylvan. I can picture you in your white coat with a stethoscope."

"That's the nicest thing any teacher ever said to me," she smiles.

I am watching Mrs. K talking and choosing books with Sylvan. I pick up a book fatter than *Jane Eyre* and ask Mrs. K if it would be good for me to read. It's called *An American Tragedy*. "Oh, that's really for my seniors, Marisol. You can try it if you like," but she sounds doubtful, as if she is assuming maybe Sylvan will accomplish her future, and I won't. A little fire is lit in me, burning against Sylvan and Mrs. K. I don't like this anger with my two best American friends, and now I'm homesick for Paloma and Nati, who supported my hopes even if Paloma's only dream is getting out of high school. Nati wants to be the first woman rocket scientist in

Mexico. That girl dreams big maybe because her father teaches at

the university and makes her do math all day on the weekends.

Nati's last name is Cho, Natividad Cho. That's pretty weird in

Tijuana, but Nati says she doesn't care. I will try to act like Nati

more often.

Besides, what would Mrs. K and Sylvan say if they

understood I have lived a tragedy. I could write the *River Ghost*

Tragedy or *Tijuana Tragedy* by Marisol de Lira Lima. So I will try to

prove my future and read *An American Tragedy*, which the back

cover tells is about murder, which probably will give me nightmares

again, but it would be worth it to prove I could read this big book.

And Mrs. K and Sylvan can take their assumptions and

write their own books. I go to my desk to start my new big book

and wait for class to begin.

The warning bell rings and most of our classmates come in,

though I notice the Jennifers are not in class. They got caught and they're probably in the office, crying like cats and dogs. People are texting and talking loud-hyper about the food fight. The tardy bell rings, and they're still being rude when Mrs. Kovacs taps on the word on the PowerPoint and then moves to the same word on the white board.

"Ah crap," says Stan. Stan is short and fat and always trying to make the class laugh. He wears his hair in a super-buzz as if he's a big athlete. When he says *crap*, the class laughs, except for me. Sylvan laughed.

"Language, please," Mrs. K smiles. "Today, you are going to write an essay."

"Duh," Stan says, and no one laughs at this rudeness.

"Get out your *Great Expectations* text."

"I knew I'd hate this book. Look at its stupid cover," says Stan.

The cover is pretty lame, the colors are too dark and the drawing is old-fashioned, but I know better than to judge a book by its cover because that's like assuming, but a little shiny on the cover

would help.

"Great Regurgitations," one of the marching band girls says.

She raises her hand, "May I use my Lark notes?"

"Lark notes are evil incarnate," Mrs. K answers. "Here is

your essay topic on the board and then on the PowerPoint. You

will have fifteen minutes to write and then we will peer edit by

reading the drafts in groups. You can use your writing name on

your draft." She lifts the overhead projector screen to reveal the

topic and clicks the computer mouse to switch the power point

screen:

Topic: *Choose one of the characters you know best. Pretend that

character was at lunch with you today. What did the character say and do?*

"Can we use swear words?" asks Stan. Stan has no restraint

unless he is surrounded by older boys. He uses RA as his writing

name as if being called Road Apple is the bomb. I use Sunny

Delamar, and Sylvan chose Forrest Glen like Forrest Gump, I

guess. Sylvan and I had fun coming up with our writing names, pseudonyms, that Stan says as pu-sway-do-nim-ees to be stupid.

"This is a first draft," Mrs. K answers like the cat who swallowed the canary since she doesn't read first drafts. Stan can write garbage all period if he wants to.

We begin writing although I have a hard time choosing, Pip or Joe or Estella? I settle on Joe because I think no one else will choose Joe, and Mrs. K will be impressed by my original thinking. Although some people make a big deal of crumpling up paper and thumbing through their books, the room is mostly quiet. When the timer goes off, we ask for more time please because the assignment is sort of fun, which I should have known it would be. Mrs. K cranks five more minutes onto the ticking timer, and the classroom carries no sound except for pens or pencils racing across paper, a sound I like.

The bing-bong-bong of the P.A. system makes us jump, and Sylvan and I look at one another, positive that they are going to start announcing more names of kids who need to report to the office. Mrs. K fluffs her hair out with her fingers and tells the class to listen.

First there's a screeching of the microphone, like always, and then Mr. Moore begins. "Students, as you know we had an unusual disruption at lunch time. Those involved have been apprehended, and the administration has dealt with them as required by our school conduct code." I kick Sylvan's chair, and she turns around to me, saying "shhhhhhhhh" and winks and adds "it."

Mr. Moore goes on. "There is now a second disruption to our day. Because of the air quality and the changing direction of the fires, the district has asked that we evacuate our school," and the cheering is so loud I cannot hear the rest. Mrs. Kovacs reads something in her email and comes to the front of the class.

"Put your writing name on your paper, turn it in, and then go to the bus loading area. All of you know your evacuation loading number." We learned these numbers on the first day of school in case of a drive-by shooting, a terrorist attack, or snow. Nobody said anything about fire back then.

Some Rivers End on the Day of the Dead

My address is Mrs. Beauman's address so I know I should go over to that group to get on that bus. Mexicans don't live in their neighborhood. None of those kids think I live near them, and they will probably rat me out. So I follow Sylvan. Neither of us has a cell phone, but I assume I can walk from her trailer before I am supposed to be home and then Mama won't worry. Sylvan hugs me when I join her in her line.

She says something about how her grandmother makes the best granola.

We get seats at the front by the bus driver, who looks like Raymond on "Everybody Loves Raymond" that my *abuela* watches on reruns. The bus driver greets kids with "Welcome aboard, sit down, and shut up." He's waiting for a few stragglers, and a super-young man teacher I don't know is counting us—he could be one of the seniors except his shirt says "staff." He's supposed to be taking roll from his list, but he skips that. Teachers probably want to get home as much as we do.

Some Rivers End on the Day of the Dead

He finishes counting and writes the number on his paper. The bus driver uses his microphone to yell, "Don't open the windows! If you're quiet, I'll turn on the radio." Everybody claps their hands and says things like "epic" and "gnarly" and "sick," words I am trying to use more when I talk in our English groups. Sylvan makes a face by raising her eyebrows and tightening her lips when I try too hard.

As he starts to close the bus's door, a sneaker the size of a bar bell is inserted into the gap, soon followed by Mr. Moore. He zooms his laser vision from back to front, focusing on each face, Zejen, kid, kid, kid, Sylvan. . . until he finds the one he wants: me.

Chapter 5: Over-exposure

Sylvan stands up. "Mr. Moore, Marisol forgot her key, and she needs to come to my house.

He rubs his nose, and for a minute, I think Sylvan is a genius.

"Sorry. Rules are rules." He points to Sylvan. "You sit down." He points to me and the bus's door. "You get on the right bus. On the way home, call your mother. Follow your family emergency plan." He doesn't even think that maybe I don't have a cell phone or a family that would make an emergency plan. I don't protest because I assume it wouldn't do any good.

Some Rivers End on the Day of the Dead

Sylvan knows when to give up. She gives me a thumb's up. "Good luck. Don't worry. See you tomorrow."

I swing my backpack from the seat and loop it over one shoulder. Mr. Moore is tapping a pencil on a clipboard. "Hurry up. You belong on Bus 12, and the whole evacuation is waiting for people like you who think this is some kind of holiday. Move it."

I get on Bus 12, which is crammed with rich kids. No one looks up from their phones, and no one moves over either. Sylvan told me that people like to ride two to a seat even though the district rule is for three to a seat and if you push in to sit three to a seat somebody will yell "homo" no matter what. The bus can't move until I sit down. Mr. Moore points his clipboard, "Right there, now!" and when I sit, he leaves, giving the bus driver a sign with a circle like he's a *caballero* swinging a lariat overhead. I find I am on the outer edge of a seat with Taljen and Shojen.

Stan yells from the back of the bus where he's sitting by the only person who would sit by Stan, a quiet boy with a pizza face. "Homo! Lezzies! Marisol, cheating on your sweetie, Sylvan?

Some Rivers End on the Day of the Dead

Marisol and Sylvan, the S and M team of all time!" Everybody

laughs except the Jens, and my face turns red.

Shojen turns on the seat to face Stan. "Just shut up! I'll

report you, you and your bully mouth." Stan shuts up.

I want to go ask Stan or the Jens what he means, but the

bus has started moving and I am too shy, and I have to wonder and

remember to tell Sylvan and Mrs. K about S and M team.

The Jens are so skinny that they don't take up much room

and our shoulders aren't even touching, much less our legs. They

show one another their phones, talking behind their hands at what

everybody's texting. Taljen says out loud, "Boys, immature brats."

I nod. I sit. I open *Great Expectations*. I barely understand

this book when I read it when I can concentrate, and now the bus is

noisy and my thoughts are noisy, and I put it away. I can't see out

the window. It's only about five minutes, every single person on

this bus, including fat Stan, should be walking to and from school,

but the district probably thinks they are keeping kids safe from the river people by having the kids ride the bus, either that or the parents made a big deal of the long walk.

The bus pulls up at the far corner from Mrs. Beauman's house. I have to stand up for the Jens to exit. I would like to get off last. I'm the ninth person off the bus, and I turn to go to Mrs. Beauman's house, but I don't want the Jens to see me there because maybe their moms are friends with Mrs. Beauman. I don't want to go to the river because if Tomaso is not home yet, I won't feel safe there, assuming men have not found work today and have come back to the river before me.

I am debating which way, which way, when Shojen stops in front of me.

"Do you live here? You haven't been on this bus before."

"Wait, what?" I stall.

"Which one is your house?"

"Umm, my aunt lives near here," I say for no reason. "I ride the other bus when I'm not at her house." That's a pretty fast lie, almost as fast as Sylvan's to Mr. Moore, like taking candy from a baby, which if anyone saw my little brothers with candy, they would know is a very stupid idiom.

"Isn't this the scariest day of your life?" Taljen asks and I can see she's crying; her mascara is running down her cheeks. "I can hardly breathe," she says, getting out her inhaler and sucking in a gasping breath. Shojen beats on her back.

They would not understand the scariest day of my life, when shots cracked the August night in our street. We all hid under the bed at *Abuela's*, trying not to breathe or move until the policemen came and said to us that Papa wasn't really investigating drugs, he was in the drug ring, which we knew was not true, but you cannot argue with policemen in Mexico. There was Mama crying, and *Abuela* crying, and my brothers and me, huddling in a circle. I hope I won't have nightmares tonight because I'm thinking of Papa's murder. Tomaso had been in Mexico, but that afternoon he returned here to Santa Dorena for a big job, he said. It seemed like a year before we reached him face-to-face although it was two days. Then Tomaso didn't cry, but he looked like a balloon without air in it. Mama and I and Tomaso missed Papa's funeral, and he says the family will make up for that on *El Dia de los Muertes*, which is not American Halloween.

The Jens hurry off without saying goodbye, they are scared to stand in this ash wilderness. Stan watches me from across the street and then disappears either into a house or around the corner. I think again about going straight to Mrs. Beauman's front door, but two cars are in the driveway. She probably is going to evacuate to Beverly Hills or Palm Springs or Malibu, somewhere television shows as wonderful.

And then a sickening thought hits me. What if she takes Mama with her? Mrs. Beauman doesn't like to take care of Andy full-time even on the weekends. She has Mama work half-days on Saturday morning and two hours on Sunday evening.

I need to get Mama alone to make a plan to meet with her again. When I sneak over to the back gate, it is locked. I slip around front, hiding behind a tall skinny cyprus tree. If anyone looked over this way, they'd see me. Sylvan could hide herself behind a cyprus tree, but not me, the *frijole* queen.

The front door opens, Mama is carrying Andy and the Beaumans, Mister and Missus, follow with about fourteen suitcases and a porta-crib and three diaper bags. Mr. Beauman goes back to the door to pick up a box of Andy's toys and begins stuffing the car and trying to shut the hatch. They don't know that Andy is happy playing with a Tupperware bowl and a wooden spoon.

"I hope we don't need the car's roof rack," Mr. Beauman says to no one.

Mama puts Andy into his car seat. This is my chance. I drop to my knees to peek and wave.

Mama nods at me and then walks around to get into the car. She says, "Missus, *por un momento*."

Mrs. Beauman is helping to stuff the hatch and gives Mama a half-hearted nod. Mama goes inside, and I want to follow so I know what to do. I begin to move towards the door.

Mr. Beauman slams the hatch by pushing against it with his shoulder. He calls out, "All aboard!"

Mrs. Beauman laughs, but it is just a laugh noise. She waits one, two, and then yells, the loudest I have ever heard her, "Auda, we have to leave NOW."

Mama bends at the waist and lifts the door mat and then rushes over to the car. As they drive away, she looks back through her window. I hope she will lean ahead and ask Mr. Beauman to stop for me.

Instead, I see her raise her hand in farewell. Tears flood my eyes, and my stomach feels like I have eaten too much too fast. I lean over, put my head between my knees, and try to breathe hard. I don't want to faint.

At least she knows I am here, I assure myself, and I rush to read the note. It has the Beauman's phone number on it and says, "*Espere a que Tomaso. Coge el dinero y los pasaportes de la lata de café. El dinero está en uno de los pañales de tela de Andy dentro de un pañuelo rojo.*

Some Rivers End on the Day of the Dead

Voy a hacer un montón de dinero extra de la Beaumans. Te amo, mi valiente Marisol, which translates like this:

Wait for Tomaso. Get the money and passports from the coffee can. The money is in one of Andy's cloth diapers inside a red kerchief. I will make a lot of extra money from the Beaumans. I love you, my brave Marisol. Mama

"My brave Marisol?" No, Mama, I am not brave, and I need you. But it is not a good time for me to break down in a tantrum like Diego, so I breathe very deeply. I focus on living in a nice apartment with a shower of our own, a toilet of our own, a kitchen. I wake up out of my day dream when more cars move down the street. I tell myself that Tomaso will take care of me until Mama comes back

I have no choice but to go to the arroyo. I pull a scarf from my backpack and I wet it with water at the Beauman's garden hose. I tie the bandana around my nose and mouth, and I cross the street.

Our arroyo is not empty even though the river ghost people who live here seem to have fled. At the far northern end, bulldozers flatten the tumbleweeds, leaving behind dusty clouds and flying sticks. The cleared arroyo is filling with small tents, firemen

of every size in every color of uniform, and fire trucks, yellow ones

and red ones, lined up.

A fireman approaches me with his funny hat under his arm.

"Off limits, miss. Walk back around the yellow tape. Get inside."

How can I tell him this is my house? How can I tell him my

house is the third oak from the left if you are counting from the

central path? How can I tell him I must check for a coffee can that

contains our only hope and that my mother has left me behind so

she can earn money by caring for a stranger's baby and that I need

to find my uncle or I will be alone?

"Yes, sir," I say, thinking that if I walk in the direction of

the apartments, I can sneak in by the fence to our tree. "Are the

apartments evacuated?"

"Not yet," he says. "We've got the fire north of here. Keep

the news on."

Some Rivers End on the Day of the Dead

I like him even if he doesn't understand my problems, and I thank him again and I plan how to get around this big mess and save our stuff and our money.

Tomaso is not where I can see him, and I keep walking past the apartments. The firemen are very busy, packing gear and loading the trucks. One by one the trucks race away with their sirens wailing. I am glad the fireman told me about the fire line to the east because to me the siren is the sound of a rainy night with Papa dying in the mud of our street.

I climb the wrought-iron fence behind the apartments and fall into the scratchy oleander bushes. There is a napoli cactus here Mama trims to use in some of the dishes she cooks. I'd laugh to watch the Beauman's faces in finding out why Mama's tamale sauce is so good from a cactus growing near where the river ghosts pee. I slap my face when I see my backpack is on the far side of the fence. Idiot! I forgot to throw it over the fence first.

No one bothers with me. I am coughing behind my kerchief. I imagine I look like a bandido, Marisol, La Zorro, just like

Some Rivers End on the Day of the Dead

Papa with his mustache! I hunch over to run to our tree. No one is there, and our few things sit in plain sight. The coffee can is buried under the tree near the fifth root, and I grab the spoon we use for beans and rice to save our can. The dirt is crumbly, not smooth.

The spoon clangs against metal, and I know I have done a good thing for Mama and Tomaso and me when I get together with them again. I pull the can up. I find our passports. I take mine and Mama's too, but there's Tomaso's green card! He hasn't come yet! I will find him. I pull out the tied-up cloth diaper. Maybe Mama forgot something because there is no red kerchief tied around it. The bundle is lighter than it should be. The knot is stuck, and I use my teeth to force it.

The money I imagined at $500, but there is only $25. Someone has taken our money, our future, our plan, our hope, my safety parachute. I stuff the twenty dollar bill and the five dollar bill into my jeans pocket, and run for the fence like a soldier in training, if soldiers have worried hearts.

Some Rivers End on the Day of the Dead

With my head down and the ashes falling harder, it is hard
to breathe.

I run smack into the police officer.

She grabs my elbow.

I pull my arm back, but she holds on. I think about dashing
away. Mama called me brave. Here is a test. Is Marisol brave, or is
that Mama's assumption?

Chapter 6: Alone

"I'm Officer Hardesty," she says as she taps her name tag. She opens her badge to show me. I wouldn't know a real badge from a pole in the ground, but I am glad she thinks this is important. "I need your name and address." She pulls a tablet out of the pocket above her breast.

She reminds me of Tomaso, all muscle except she has some curves, and a laughing mouth with a crooked tooth where Tomaso has the gap and the gold tooth. Her hair is cut short; her bangs are reddish-brown. Even though she is an officer, her eyes reflect softness instead of the dull, hardness I saw in the eyes of the Mexican policemen who came after Papa died.

Some Rivers End on the Day of the Dead

She writes down what I tell her, the Beauman's address and my writing name, Sunny Delamar, that I dreamed up with Sylvan. The silliness of that lunch-time seems to have happened a thousand years ago to a different girl than me.

"Did your family evacuate?"

"My mother is downtown. We'll meet at the center. That's our family emergency plan." These lies slip out easily, and I wonder how I have become a good liar so fast. Then I think of all the lies I have told about where I live, or not lies, but omissions, and I know I have been living a lie, a river ghost's life. I need to remember Papa's key word: *restraint*.

"I'll drive you to the evacuation center."

"My backpack's over there. My school books, you know?" I point to where I tossed it. "Let me get my stuff."

"I bet you're a good student."

And a liar, I think. When I get to where my backpack should be, it's gone. My wallet with my school i.d. card and notes from Sylvan are in it, and now gone. Whoever took the backpack threw my math book and my *Great Expectations* on the ground.

I come back to the patrol car with my two books. Officer Hardesty has typed the information I gave her into her computer. My writing name must not have come up on a wanted list or a terrorist list—I think it sounds like a movie star even though Stan says it sounds more like a porn star-- because she tells me to buckle up and asks, "No backpack?"

I show her the books. "Just these."

Officer Hardesty scans the yellow-taped river area to see if there are other people who need help or maybe she is looking for the backpack thief. A bus has arrived to take all the old people from the apartments with their wheel chairs and oxygen tanks. The drug addicts melted into the street crowd at the bus stop in a New-York minute. I wonder if there is also an LA minute and a Tijuana minute. One of my *Abuela's* Tijuana minutes would be much longer than a New York minute. Officer Hardesty speaks into her walkie-

Some Rivers End on the Day of the Dead

talkie, "J-11-29. Transporting juvenile to Smiley Canyon evac center," and the word *juvenile* is like a pinch to wake up.

Juvenile. I wish she had said a name. Everything I know about juveniles has to do with delinquents and the honor ranch that is the jail for bad kids.

She doesn't turn the siren on, and my heart's hammering slows down.

She drives north up the freeway and gets off near the amusement park I've heard about. I strain my neck trying to see the tallest roller coaster in Los Angeles. We arrive at Smiley Canyon School, and she comes around to lead me inside. I would rather stay with Officer Hardesty, but I understand that she has more work to do and probably juvenile delinquents to deal with. We walk in, her hand on my elbow like a friend, except the firmness means control. She must feel it's in me to run. A crowd is in the big auditorium, some people in line for food and some people filling in forms. It is noisy with crying babies and chasing children, and I really do not want to be here.

Some Rivers End on the Day of the Dead

"Sign these forms and choose a cot over there, Sunny." Officer Hardesty turns to leave. I see a sign that says "women and families" with dividers set up. Another area is for "men," and I will check in that area for Tomaso, unless he is already looking in the family area for me.

"Thank you, officer," I say. "I'll be okay." Another lie.

I fill in the forms, and I write that my name is Sunny Delamar in case the gang men, the horrible men from Mexico, have spies here. I hand the forms to the worker at the table. He is an older, skinny priest with trimmed red hair and veins across his cheeks and nose. He is from a church we don't go to. "*Se habla español?*"

"I speak English," I tell him. "I am a full U.S. citizen."

He raises his eyebrows. His yellow front teeth gnaw his lip while he thinks.

"We'll keep you safe until we can reach your-- um-- mother," he assures me as he reads my forms. "Are you hungry?"

He points me to the food line.

Some Rivers End on the Day of the Dead

"Will you tell me if my Uncle Tomaso Lira is here or comes here?" I should not have said that. They say gangs pay off even some priests. He doesn't write the name down, only nods okay.

I wait and wait. When it's my turn, I choose a pack of chips, two apples, orange Jello, and a bottle of water. It's not much. I'm tired. When I have Mama or Tomaso, the world doesn't feel so heavy on my shoulders. The whole crazy morning-- Mr. Moore and the bus-- seeing my mother wave goodbye. No Tomaso, no backpack, it's too much for a fourteen-year old girl by herself. I wish Nati or Paloma or Sylvan were here with me. If I got to choose, I would choose Paloma because she is always laughing. We served many detentions with Sister Ignacio for our classroom giggling. Nati is more serious and ironic, like Sylvan except Sylvan likes to move all the time, wiggling her foot during every class. Nati can sit still for hours. She won the who-won't-laugh staring contest in seventh grade. Nati's high cheekbones and narrow eyes never flinched.

Some Rivers End on the Day of the Dead

I find a cot in the family section off in the second row where no one else has their stuff. Each cot has a blanket, and it's cold in the auditorium from the air-conditioning. I take off my school shirt glad that I have a tank top underneath. I put the school shirt over my eyes to block out all these people, all this noise, all this stuff I don't want to see. I tuck the blanket up as far as my chin, thinking of Mama. I sleep, hoping Tomaso comes soon even though I will then have to tell him about the missing money and watch his face harden from a smile to his angry look.

I awaken because it is quiet, not quiet like the dry river with leaves and wind and our neighbor river ghosts, but quiet like sleeping people. The crying babies have been soothed, the toddlers are worn out, the others, like me, are curled into their cots with their blankets over them. I am hungry and want to eat my apples without big crunching sounds. I go into the restroom and wash my hands before eating to prevent a disease like polio or ebola virus that Papa's encyclopedias taught me about.

Some Rivers End on the Day of the Dead

"See, Papa. I follow your advice," I say to myself in the bathroom mirror. My image looks scruffy. I comb my fingers through my hair and wish for Mrs. Beauman's shower and her Ivory soap. Why didn't I stay there? I would like to cry, but there is no use drowning in my own tears the way Alice did in the book Papa read to me that I told him I didn't like. I told him it was boring, but it wasn't boring. It was scary. If there is a rabbit hole to fall down, I have done that.

I wash my hands again, splash water on my face, and eat one apple and my orange Jello that makes me think of Sylvan, and I wonder when I will get to laugh with Sylvan again, if ever. How did my life become one big mess? I sit in the corner of the bathroom against the cold tiles, wondering what will happen tomorrow if Tomaso isn't here for me or if he comes and I'm in the bathroom will he just leave? This thought drops one more bad feeling into my stomach, and I return to my cot. I will lose myself in the story of *Great Expectations* even though there is barely enough light to read.

Some Rivers End on the Day of the Dead

When I am reading, I think about Pip, the orphan, and then about myself without Mama or Tomaso. Tomaso is smart, not book smart like Papa, but street smart, like the scary man, Magwich in the book. Tomaso can use a knife or his fists. He will find out where all of the river ghosts have gone. He will come to this place for me, and Mama will return from Malibu or Beverly Hills and we will live a better life if the Beaumans pay Mama her money or the same life if they don't, at least until it rains. Why was it that I found so little of our money safe? Why was there not a red handkerchief?

One day this time will be so much water under the bridge, which reminds me of rivers. Next time, we'll choose another branch of a better river, as Mama promised, as Papa said. Like Mrs. K, I have great expectations for myself, expectations for me, Marisol. I close my eyes and sleep.

A baby cries, a cart with squeaky wheels clacks in, and all around me I hear coughing and farting and early morning noises. I do not want to get up around all these strangers. I wish I had known even one of the other river ghost women to feel a part of a group. Chairs are dragged across the gym floor with a screech, and my head aches. This must be the way Tomaso's head aches after too much tequila on pay days or when he has a black eye after fighting. Another dream I have is that Tomaso will marry and move away so that mama can quit worrying about him. Mrs. K calls the Jens flighty. I call Tomaso fighty. I need him, but a better him.

The overhead lights flare on. I put the blanket over my head so that I am sitting on my cot like a ghost on what the Americans call Halloween, which comes one day before our Day of the Dead. Under the blanket, I pull on my school shirt, which still smells okay except the smoky smell. What am I going to do without a shower and deodorant today? The thought of being stinky while the Jens and the Brittanys are fresh from their showers makes me angry. I could have stayed in the Beauman's nice house with the warm water and comfortable beds if I had thought about it for two minutes, to go through a window, or if Mama had left a key instead of me running off to the oak trees and Mama in the back seat of the Beauman's car waving goodbye. I pinch my arm because my family is so stupid.

I throw the blanket down on the cot and walk to the door. A nun who is not the famous Mother Nun in "The Sound of Music" stops me. "No one leaves here without a pass, and no kids leave without parents," she tells me.

"A pass?"

"Your parent has to sign out the family."

"My mama?" I am acting stupid because my head hurts so much and maybe my heart hurts too.

"We have to follow procedures," she says, and her eyes look sharp, like a hawk's. I can't get out this door unless she takes a break. Tomaso will come by then.

I wait in line for some breakfast, a mush that should be called goat meal. Lots of sugar improves the flavor. My headache gets smaller. I check the door. Hawk nun sees me spying on her so I turn away and go into the bathroom. It is crowded in there with the babies getting their diapers changed, and the stink brings the headache back, sharp and hard.

My cot creaks to greet me as my home now, the way the oak trees creaked in the wind of the river valley. I never thought I would miss a sleeping bag under an oak tree and my bathroom of oleander bushes. I lie down on one elbow and begin reading my book. I am happy to go with Pip to London where he is spending money too fast and joking about how many bills he has to pay. Pip is not very smart about money, not like Mama. Even Tomaso knows how to save for a rainy day, I hope. In our world, a rainy day is the day we will need cash, but then I remember our saved money is gone, or most of it is, and I wish I could eat a piece of mushroom like Alice did and all of a sudden I would be a grown up with all the answers.

I read and read. I should have post-its to mark questions so I tear up scraps from the edge of Mama's note, and seeing the note makes me choke out a sad sound, guh. The paper is not as colorful as Sylvan's flags, but I am not as colorful as Sylvan either. I concentrate on Mr. Dickens' story, trying to forget my problems and finally losing myself in the idea of being Pip.

From behind, someone puts hands over my eyes. I expect this person to say, "Guess who?'" No sound except the gym sounds, the people sounds. I reach up to the hands to feel if the hands are rough like Tomaso's. Who else could it be?

The hands are smooth and small, and my heart leaps. It must be Mama. She has come back for me! But the hands do not have Mama's scent of cinnamon and baby powder. I smell orange soda.

When I push the hands away and turn my head, in back of me is not Mama. But there is still a sight for my very sore eyes: Sylvan.

Chapter 7: Where Now?

Sylvan and I screech like the emo Jens, hugging one another. My eyes fill with tears, and Sylvan hands me a crumpled tissue out of her hoodie's pocket.

"Why are you here?" I ask when we both sit on my cot.

"The fire crossed the ridge, and the trailer park totally burned. Granny and I put a ton of crap in the car, and here we are!" Sylvan is chewing her green hair ends, and the way it is pulled across her lip looks like a mustache. I push her hand down so that she won't chew her hair. Chewing hair makes split ends according to my *abuela.*

"Where's your grandmother?" I ask, looking around for an old, white lady with big hips.

"She's filling out forms." Sylvan stands on her tip toes and stretches up to see if she can see her grandmother. "Don't you watch the news, Marisol?" Sylvan gestures toward the television sets in the four corners of the auditorium, each one surrounded by dozens of people. Little kids are yelling for cartoons, but the adults look serious.

"Sleeping and reading."

"Where's your mom?"

"Working." I can't tell Sylvan that Mama left me behind for money because I know the feeling in my stomach will climb up to my throat, and these drops of tears will become a river.

"Bummer. God, did you hear about our school?"

"Our school?"

"It burned down. The whole thing. Gone. I bet everybody except us is cheering." Sylvan is jiggling her feet. "I swear I can hear Road Apple laughing from here. Can you?"

I wish I could laugh.

"I hope Mrs. K is safe," Sylvan adds.

"Where will we go to school if our school is gone? Will we keep our teachers? Do you think we'll still be reading this book?" I am asking too many questions, but if I don't keep talking, I'll melt like the witch in that movie. Maybe we should watch the news to see what's going on. Maybe the burned school is really another school, not our school, not Mrs. K's school.

Sylvan shakes her head. She's not laughing, but she points her toes, sitting still. "A schedule comes out today. They have to make plans. Our valley is one big mess."

"What if they cancel school all year?"

"They can't. The state pays money for us. That's why they care about attendance and why they're so mad about senior ditch days."

Sylvan is a much more original thinker than I am; she watches the news and reads a newspaper and talks to her granny about politics. I thought school was school to make sure we're not stupid and slow as molasses. I didn't know American school had to do with money except what kids wear for shoes and what kids have for showing off, like video games and other phone apps.

"Look, here comes my grandmother!" Sylvan points at a lady with short silver hair that is gelled back over her ears. I can see the tracks of comb marks in the hair. She wears feather earrings that hang from her ear lobes to her chin. She's has on tight black jeans, a red western shirt, and a tie like Tomaso wears to a wedding, a bolo. Her hips are narrow, and I would never call her hippy. She looks much too young to be called Granny.

"Granny! Marisol is here! Her mother isn't. She can stay with us, can't she? How long are we going to be here? What's happening with our new school? Did you get money?" Sylvan's words come out in such a rush that her grandmother draws her hand across her lips in the sign Coach Sneed makes for zip your lips.

Teenagers use slang codes, and adults use hand motions.

Some Rivers End on the Day of the Dead

Sylvan's grandmother plunks a straw basket purse onto the floor. Then she reaches out to hug Sylvan and she pulls me close as well. Her hands are tanned and calloused. She wears a ring on each finger of her left hand and a toe ring on the toe next to her big toe.

"Hello. What did Miss Chatterbox say your name was?" she asks me in a voice that sounds rough and scratchy like those old singers who stay too long in their careers, Barry Manilope, Tomaso called the one of them.

"I'm Marisol. Marisol de Lira Lima. I am registered here as Sunny Delamar . .. because that was our family's emergency plan. You know, a family code."

"Good idea, a family code. Call me Granny Linda or just Linda."

Sylvan butts in with "Granny, Granny, Granny, tell us! What's your plan?" Granny pushes the blanket, my books, and Sylvan's backpack onto the floor to join her purse, and pats the open area of the cot. Sylvan and I both sit.

"School won't re-open for two weeks. They're saying you'll go to Viewpoint High School. Where's that?" Sylvan and I shrug. "Your school has mornings, the Viewpoint kids go afternoons. You'll ride buses from the new housing center."

"What's that mean?" Sylvan is bouncing on the cot and her granny holds Sylvan's shoulders.

"You worry too much. Every day is a gift, no matter what it brings." Granny Linda gazes across the auditorium, but her eyes are blurry. "We'll always have more than we need."

"What about Marisol? What should she do? What if she can't find her family?" Sylvan hugs me. "She like totally so needs us."

I cross my eyes at her over-Jen Jen language.

"I don't know." Granny Linda looks me in the eyes, and I must look as pitiful as Pip because she decides. "We could sign her out. The city wants to empty this center soon. We'll drive to Ventura. I have friends with room for us."

It all sounds like a smooth maneuver to me, but I am worried. "I don't think I should leave, Mrs. Granny. I should wait for my mama or my uncle. Tomaso could be here right now looking for me."

"Go check the lists. And while you girls do that, I'll make calls." She pulls a phone out of her purse. It is completely wicked to see a grandmother with a hot pink phone.

Sylvan and I approach the tables, searching the crowd for other kids we might know from school. I'm hoping and not hoping to see Tomaso. We wave a small finger wave at some other free lunch kids, and then we wait and wait in line while a lady speaks to the red-haired priest. She is going on and on about food stamps and housing for five children and the mother and the father, and I feel very lucky to have found Sylvan and her smart Granny, who uses a cell phone and knows how to manage this system.

When it's our turn, I'm afraid to ask about Tomaso because even though I do want him here, not lost, and I don't want him worrying about me, I also don't want him here because going with

Sylvan and her grandmother would be much more fun than sitting around listening to Tomaso's singing and having to cook for him and worrying about him drinking and fighting without my Mama there in the new city trailers. I can use Granny Linda's phone to leave a message on the Beauman's phone so that Mama won't worry.

The priest has been waiting, tapping his pencil against his yellow teeth. My lips are zipped because my mouth is so dry, and Sylvan says, "My friend needs to know if her family has checked in yet."

"Okay," he says. "Names?"

Sylvan waits for me to answer, and when I don't, she gives my back a little pinch, right where the flabby part hangs over my jeans waistband.

"Tomaso. Tomaso Lima," I say. "Remember, I asked you to tell me if he came in looking for me?" The priest shrugs. What if Tomaso used a fake name too? Maybe I should ask about Mama, but I know she's with the Beaumans so what's the use?

Some Rivers End on the Day of the Dead

The priest turns a clipboard towards us. Sylvan runs

through pages to the L's and the T's. Tomaso is not listed. She

runs her finger down the lists again, this time one by one, carefully,

and shows me. "He's not here."

"I wonder where he is," I say in barely a whisper, and now

my head hurts and my stomach too. What if he is still at the river?

What if another officer or Officer Hardesty took him away because

he didn't get his green card? I flip some pages to see if there are any

names that might be a fake name for Tomaso. I don't know how

he would think.

Granny Linda returns to where we are. "Any luck?"

I shake my head no, but the shaking hurts my eyes.

"Granny Linda, could I use your phone?" She hands it right over.

I reach into my pocket for Mama's note and type in the numbers

with shaky fingers. When the answering machine comes on, it

beeps and Mrs. Beauman's soft voice says, "Sorry we missed you.

Leave a message, and please speak slowly." She says the word *slow* as slow as molasses pouring. Before there's a beep, a mechanical voice announces, "This mail box is full." I shut the phone off.

"No use." I am so sad.

"What's wrong?" Sylvan asks and pats my arm.

"The mailbox is full, no more messages allowed."

"Just leave a note here."

I write the note and give it to the list priest. I have written Tomaso Lima on the outside of the folded note. What else can I do? Sylvan gives her granny the phone back even though I can tell she'd like to keep it for herself because she sort of palmed it until her granny put her hand out for it.

We wait in line to use the toilets and then the sinks. The bathroom smells of a heavy cleaner, but it is not enough to cover up the dirty people smell and the baby diaper smell. One of the toilets has leaked water all over the floor, and I want to wash my shoes in the sink except I don't want to stand barefoot on this gross floor.

Some Rivers End on the Day of the Dead

I splash cold water onto my face, wishing this was not
happening, to be back under my oak near the river or in the
Beaumans kitchen even if I was doing ten pages of math homework
with x's and y's and people going both ways on a river at different
speeds, and I had to solve for where they would meet. I wish I
could solve where they would meet right now.

And then we go out to pick up all our stuff off the cot,
including the blanket and Sylvan's backpack and my two books. I
ask Sylvan if she has an aspirin. She digs through backpack, opens
a bottle, and hands me one, which I swallow dry, the bitter taste
waking me up more. She puts the aspirin back into a yellow wallet
thing with black polka dots. That's where she keeps her box of
tampons just in case too.

Granny Linda signs a form at the desk, and they don't even
question that I am leaving with her.

Outside, the wind is blowing hard, pelting us with bits of
weeds and fine sand from the playing fields. We hold on tightly to
one another's shirts, our heads down, as we make our way to a

dented pink Toyota. Flower-power decals decorate the sides, big purple daisies and a loopy, fat script like graffiti on the freeway. It says "Fun, fun, fun, Go Linda Go."

As the sand hits my face and I gaze at the car, I get it. Hippie like Grateful Dead. Hippie like San Francisco and Haight-Ashbury from Discovery Channel and Mr. McKee's class. Stupid, Marisol. You are stupid about English words, especially if you just hear them and don't read them. No wonder Papa spent so much time explaining to me. I hope I find Mrs. Kovacs again soon because I have a long list of idioms for tutoring in American English.

Granny Linda, the hippie lady, opens the car's trunk and leans with both hands on it to keep it from flying off. When our stuff is stuffed in, Sylvan and I buckle up in the backseat. Sylvan asks, "How long to Ventura, Granny?"

Granny glances into the rearview mirror. She shakes her head. "My friend's phone was disconnected. We'll have to go to plan B. Who has a Plan B?"

Some Rivers End on the Day of the Dead

Why is she asking us? She should be in charge, like Mrs. K or even Mr. Moore or Coach Sneed. We sit. The air around us is gray and ashy, and Granny begins coughing hard. I think of safe places, clean-air places, far away from this burning valley.

"Granny Linda," I say, "I have a Plan B. It's complicated and requires original thinking." And I tell her about my *abuela's* house in Tijuana, which means we need papers for crossing the border.

Granny Linda says, "Maybe. How much money do you have, Marisol?"

I tell her I have the twenty-five dollars. Mama would understand my spending that, and I hope Tomaso has the rest although then why didn't he leave more for me and why didn't he take his green card? The answer to this question is unknown thief, and I don't want to think about it.

Granny Linda makes a phone call and nods her head, saying "He says it's $50 each. I'll cover the extra for now."

"I have my passport, Granny Linda, so maybe I will be no cost."

"Right on," she says, and she floors the gas pedal to get moving, laying down rubber the way the senior hot shots do at school with lots of noise. People at the door of the center are pointing at us. Laying down rubber must be a good car skill.

We make it to the freeway entrance, and Granny slows down for the stop-lighted on-ramp. "You two will need to keep your traps shut at the border crossing. Speak only when you're spoken to, okay Ms. Chatterbox?" She says this to Sylvan. She means me too.

The word *trap* worries me. If it's like zip your lip, I know I am good at that. I want to borrow the phone back to call my *abuela* because she likes surprises about as much as she likes the idea of a young girl who thinks she's *el queso grande* for being an American citizen and having a famous father. My *abuela* doesn't understand that nothing is so *grande* as Tomaso said it was in America. Why would I have believed a man who thinks a fake gold front tooth makes him handsome?

No wonder my father preferred his work for *El Nationale* in Tijuana compared to the job he was offered in Chula Vista, just north of the border. But would he have died in Chula Vista? If he reported the same way, yes, he would have, and that's why I am Sunny Delamar. Now I am not only a lost river ghost, but a lost river ghost with a fake name that no one knows is missing, running off with a hippie grandma and a green-haired girl. Mr. Dickens could write a story about me. Who would believe a story like that?

Besides, the great Mr. Dickens is dead too.

Chapter 8: Road Trip

It's selfish to delay our trip, but I want to leave Mama a note at the Beaumans. Granny says okay. She gets off at the next off-ramp. I describe the location of the Beauman's house, explaining where the river bridge is and how close it is to school. Streams of traffic are inching towards the freeway to get out of town; the streets going toward school are empty. As we come up the main street to turn toward the river, I wonder if I can run into the field for one more search for Tomaso, or maybe the thief had a change of heart (I picture a heart transplant like on Discovery Channel) and he brought our money back. The air has thickened with ash, and the smell of burning is everywhere. Our family oak tree appears safe. Across the way, white smoke still puffs like *Abuela's* sheets in the wind before a rainstorm. That's the only time *Abuela* moves fast, that and getting to church on Sunday. But where the smoke puffs is where our school once was.

"Let's go over to the school too," says Sylvan.

"Hush, Missy. We need to roll, more sightseeing can wait."

At the corner that intersects the Beauman's street and the river valley and our oak tree, a striped barricade stands guard with a cop car next to it. The police car's lights flash, red-blue, red-blue.

"They've closed this off. Can't get in, Marisol," says Sylvan.

"Maybe if we asked the officer?"

"People treat adults better than they treat kids. I'll ask. Give me the note, honey," says Granny Linda.

She walks over to the police car. The officer lowers the window as he unfolds out of the car. He is a tall man. Granny is pointing over to the houses, and the officer shakes his head. She shows him the note, and he takes it. She turns back to the car, her hands open, shoulders shrugged.

Some Rivers End on the Day of the Dead

"He said he'd try to put it in their mail box. No guarantees so let's go."

Granny joins the cars driving north, and I know the border is south of Los Angeles and Los Angeles is south of Santa Dorena, and the far edge of Santa Dorena is south of here. I wait ten minutes as she takes a narrow road that says "to Fillmore." I don't think we want to go to Fillmore.

Sylvan traces her toes on the back window, as if she is just lying there considering the eucalyptus trees along the road and the places where citrus groves have been leveled, the tree roots drying in dusty fields like dead starfish.

I push her hair behind her ears, out of her face.

"What?" Sylvan sounds grumpy. I should leave her alone.

"We're going the wrong way."

"And you know that because. . .?"

"I read the signs."

Granny pulls the car over where there's a fruit stand. It has a tin roof and is open all the way across the front though the interior is shady and deep. Rows and rows of fruit and vegetables are set out on tables, watermelons in pyramids and soft drink refrigerators line the walls. A girl in a tank top and jeans who could be my sister with her black hair and dark eyes and chubby tummy is working the cash register.

"Trust me, Marisol," Granny Linda says.

She heard me complaining, and I am too embarrassed to talk. I mumble yes, yes, I do trust her even though she is not family and she is not taxes. I am worried about assuming this is the right thing to do.

"There is a freeway closed going south. The fires are too close and we can't drive through them unless Wonder Woman here would suggest trying that. We'll get to the coast-- take the 101." She ruffles my hair before she gets out of the car. "You okay with that? Satisfied?"

"I'm sorry to be so much trouble," I tell her. "I talk too much," and she laughs and inclines her head toward Sylvan. Since we're stopped, I ask for her phone to call *Abuela.* She says sure and leaves us in the car while she goes in to buy some fruit and nuts. After the yucky meal at the center, I picture peeling a fresh orange, taste the sticky juice. But first the call to *Abuela*.

I am nervous and drop the phone. Sylvan hands it back.

"Have you lost your mind, Marisol? This is fun. Live a little. My granny wasn't born yesterday." I must look puzzled because she says, "That means she knows what she's doing."

"I know." I am stalling. I don't know what to say to *Abuela*. I don't want her upset about Tomaso and Mama and the evacuation.

I dial the international code plus the area code plus the phone number. The phone rings and rings and rings. I am worried that she is off to the market with my brothers. I decide to count twenty rings. It is possible that she is only outside hanging up the wash on the clothes line or sitting in the courtyard with Diego and Hermes rattling in circles on their Big Wheel trikes.

At last the phone is answered. The connection rattles and cracks and whines. *"Buenos Dias! Allo?"*

Some Rivers End on the Day of the Dead

It is a man's voice. I can barely hear him. I am afraid.
What if it is the policemen again? What if *Abuela* is a suspect in
drug crimes like they said about my father?

"*Éste es Marisol. Donde está la abuela?*"

The connection clears. "Marisol!" the voice chimes like a
song. "Tomaso here! Where are you? "

I laugh and cry and tell him my story of Mama, the coffee
can money and the center, and now Sylvan and Mrs. Granny.

"So, uh, did you remember my green card?"

"No, I left it. You don't you have it? I couldn't find the red
handkerchief. I thought you would get those, and me, too, Uncle."
It seems that he doesn't have the money.

"Aye yi yi." He sighs heavily. "Uh, I thought you'd go with
your mom. No kerchief?" He stops with a heavy sigh. "Felipe and
me, we came straight here in his truck before the freeway shut
down. Never mind the green card--I have extras." He is quiet a
moment and then says shhh to the noisy room, noisy with men and
television. "Get a foster paper for you. Let me talk to the lady."

Some Rivers End on the Day of the Dead

Tomaso sounds hurried, which is not anything Tomaso is known for unless it's Friday and quitting time near a bar.

"She's in the store, but her name is . . . " I look at Sylvan who adds, "Linda Deford" into the phone. "She has friends to help us."

"We'll be waiting for you," says Tomaso. "It will be okay." He asks for Granny's phone number and then tells me, "Twenty dollars for your foster papers, no rip off prices. Use your smart head, Marisol."

"Yes, Uncle," I say as he hangs up.

Sylvan hugs me. "Good job! We'll have fun. You'll love my grandma. I hope she buys chips, soda pop, and Twinkies." Then she laughs at her own joke. I know about what Sylvan eats at school and what she eats at home, that Mrs. Granny likes natural foods only. "You're so lucky, Marisol. You have a normal family."

"You think my family is normal?"

"Yes, American normal."

"And your family is not?"

Some Rivers End on the Day of the Dead

Sylvan slumps against the seat with her elbows on the seat back, staring out the back window, tracing the painted petals of the flowers on Granny's car. The flowers say something about Mrs. Granny.

I am thinking how my normal mama left her daughter behind, but Sylvan doesn't have a mom around or a dad? Does a normal family mean having a dead dad? We wait a few minutes, and Sylvan starts to open the car door to go in and to buy something her grandmother won't like her to have.

I say, "Wait."

"Are you coming? What do you want me to get you?" She puts out her hand for change.

"It's not that. Where are your parents, Sylvan?" I have finally asked this after so many weeks of not knowing.

"I don't know. They don't write to me." Sylvan twists the friendship bracelet we made with thread in art. Hers is three shades of green; mine is aqua and navy and sky blue.

"How old were you when you moved to your granny's?"

Some Rivers End on the Day of the Dead

"I don't know--little. I don't remember any other parents except Granny." Before I can tell her about the river camp, Sylvan flings open the car door and runs to help Granny carry bags. What she bought is in bags Granny took into the store with her. I hop out to make room because the trunk is stuffed. Sylvan hands me one dollar and says "orange soda." I leave to buy sodas. I hope Granny doesn't think I am making trouble, and I wish there had been time to tell Sylvan the truth of how I have been living.

When I get back, Granny is revving the engine and drinking a beer, and we leave the fruit stand in a crunch of gravel and a swirl of dust. Granny eyes us drinking our soda and clinks her beer bottle against the steering wheel, saying "Happy Festivus." She gulps some beer and shivers her shoulders. "Don't think you'll be swilling chemicals every day, you two." The beer bottle clunks as she tosses it to the floorboards. Papa told me people should not drink and drive, and I don't like our car with a drinking driver.

The orange soda tickles my throat, fizzy and cool. Sylvan burps a huge burp for a skinny girl, and I can smell the orange soda she drank in three long swallows. Then Granny erupts with a long "brrrrrrrrrrrrrrrrrp." We all get the giggles.

"Belching is good for you. Belching and farting, natural bodily reactions. Listen to your bodies," she says. My *abuela* will have some manners training for Mrs. Granny, Mrs. Deford or vice visa, whatever that idiom is.

Granny turns the radio on to a music station that is playing wild, throbbing music. "That's Janis. Doesn't her voice make you want to shout?"

Sylvan groans, "Yeah, shout shut up!"

"Janis who? Jackson?"

"Joplin, dummy. God Marisol, you are such a retard." Sylvan punches my arm a little hard.

"That's not a nice word. Remember our assembly about bullies?" I want to punch her back.

Granny pays no attention because she is singing with Janis and pounding her palms on the steering wheel. I like this music, with big drums, crying guitar, and a woman shrieking of her life of pain. I should write a song for my pain.

I start thinking how Sylvan sits near me because our names are close in the alphabet and how lucky we are to be friends and how lucky I am to have a friend when my family is all split up and then I wonder about her mother and father, if they are somewhere she could find them again or if they are dead like my father. And I realize that Sylvan lives with her father's mother because her name is Deford and Sylvan's last name is Deford so where is her mother's family and why don't they have her? She must feel as left behind as I do except her mother has been gone longer. Her mother never came back. What if Mama never comes back to me? I would die. This will not happen. I cross myself and say a prayer to St. Christopher for safe travels although Sister Jacinta said his status has been questioned as being not even an official saint. The Church questions weird things.

I will find out more about during this trip, especially on the Day of the Dead, which is less than two weeks away. We will have our celebration for my Papa, and I will spend time instructing

Sylvan so that she won't be the only smart one about everything in

the whole world, there will be something I know that she doesn't

and if she messes up, I'll punch her arm hard, but I won't even

think the R word. I'll also be listening, like a little picture with big

ears because I am ready to learn more about our traditions finally in

my life. My ear is big, especially the ear lobe part where I will wear

pearl earrings on my *quinceañera* next May. Who will dance with me?

Granny makes the transition from the small road to a big

freeway. Traffic is slow. I am drowsy. Sylvan too. She falls asleep

with a pillow against the door, and I lean against her smooth, skinny

legs, trying to imagine who is dancing with me because it cannot be

my elegant Papa, and Tomaso would never agree. Tomaso likes

only the slow dancing, the man's front gyrating against the girl's

butt. He watched MTV until *Abuela* said no more, not in her house.

Something smells familiar, hot oil frying tacos, fresh fruit,

flowers, exhaust of buses. People are talking in Spanish. Have we already crossed the border? Does Granny need directions? I shake

my head awake and stretch my arms and legs, trying not to wake up

Sylvan.

"Where are we?" I lean forward to whisper to Granny

Linda.

"Downtown L.A."

"It feels like Tijuana."

"Little El Salvador—LA also has Little Baja, Little Oaxaca,

Little Saigon—Little anything. Beautiful city, LA."

"It's crowded here, not like Santa Dorena."

"Santa Dorena is a white ghetto."

"Ghetto?"

"Like a walled city where only certain people live."

I picture the walls around the Beauman's house. Mrs.

Granny has chosen the right image for Santa Dorena. But I

remember the ghetto was a bad thing in *The Diary of Anne Frank*. I

don't want to think of Santa Dorena in a bad way since it is and is

not my home.

Granny turns the steering wheel hard and urges the car into a parking space in front of a laundromat. She says, "Wait here. I'll be right back."

Sylvan wakes up with a cranky "God, what now?"

"Downtown LA. Little El Salvador?"

"No kidding."

"You've been here before?"

"Only about a thousand times. Granny helps too much."

Granny returns to the car and says, "Come in, girls. The man needs pictures."

"I have my passport, Granny Linda. But my uncle says you need a foster paper."

She walks in front of us, and again I think how small her butt is. I never saw such a small butt in jeans on an older lady. Even the cheerleader gym teacher couldn't wear such small jeans. "I know what we need. But this man wants your birthday and all that for the custody paper."

"Custard?" I am thinking flan, and my stomach rumbles.

"Re-," Sylvan stops herself and then pronounces the other word by syllables: "Cus-to-dy. That means it's okay for Granny to take us across the border. It's some new law from kidnappings and 9/11 or something."

We follow Granny inside. Women in t-shirts and jeans and women in the colorful clothing of El Salvador, bright skirts and off-the-shoulder tops, are sitting in rows of chairs. They are watching the dryers go around with the clothes spinning a story with their swirls of color. On the floor, a fat brown baby with big brown eyes is lying on a blanket in his diaper and a shirt that doesn't cover his tummy. Two toddlers are driving tiny plastic cars around the baby, up and over his legs. The baby giggles and laughs deep from his belly. I smile because I will see my little brothers soon.

At the counter, a Korean man is writing on a pad of paper as Granny Linda dictates information to him. She motions us to the green stools by the counter where Sylvan and I sit and wait.

"Where's your father?" Granny asks the man.

"Overseas." He doesn't look up. The man asks questions, name, parent's name, date-of-birth, city, state, country of birth. I show him my passport, and he says, "This is good."

"How long in Mexico?" he asks Granny. A strong odor of garlic comes out of his mouth. I see the kimchi on a plate next to him. He offers Granny a piece which she takes and chews with smacking sounds, and now she is going to make the car smell all the way to Tijuana. "Girls? Want one?" she asks us with a snap in her eyes. My papa's eyes held that look when he was going to play a trick on me. Besides, Nati's father is Mr. Cho, a Korean man I admire almost as much as I admire my Papa, and Mr. Cho already taught me about kim chi.

Sylvan grabs the kim chi, nibbles at it and starts slapping the counter and then holding her throat. I say no thank you.

The Korean man is wearing a gold earring. His hair is spiky, and now that we are up close, I can see he must be in his twenties. He looks like Nati's older brother, Peter (he won't use Pedro). This man has on a black rock band t-shirt for Bono, and I wonder if he's emo. His arms ripple with muscles and tattoos that look like rings

of barbed wire. Across the street there's a gym, and I bet he works

out every day. I didn't know there was so much money to be made

from laundry machines and documents.

Behind the counter, he takes a picture of Granny, Sylvan,

and me, one by one. He tells us not to smile, appear serious in the

photo. The big black umbrella makes me think of the rainy night

Papa died, and it is not hard to look serious. He prints the pictures,

pastes Sylvan and Granny's into passport booklets and mine on a

letter he has typed. He signs everything in several places, once with

his right hand and once with his left hand. He asks Granny to sign.

"Two hundred dollars, please," he tells us.

My mouth gets dry, and I am glad I didn't eat kim chi,

because I would throw up. Or maybe Granny has the rest.

"Two hundred dollars?" Granny asks.

I pat my pockets, front and back, even though this is fake

looking for money. Tomaso said more than twenty dollars would be

a rip off. "I thought it was less."

Granny tells the Korean man, "Just a minute."

She walks me to the door. "We can bargain a little, but we can't go at all without these papers. You've got how much again?"

"I told you. Twenty-five dollars. But twenty is what is fair."

"Get it out."

I hand her twenty dollars that I had ready in one pocket. "Do you think this is enough?"

"No."

I would not give away more of Mama's money even if I had it, the money she would have bought things for our new apartment, beds and mattresses and a couch, and maybe a new dress for her. I am angry with myself and angry with Granny Linda because she should have planned.

The Korean man barters the price for a few more minutes with Granny Linda, she puts the money out on the counter bill by bill. He taps each of the papers and the bills, and pulls the papers back towards him.

Granny leans across and asks if that's his final offer.

He grins like a diablo and makes a circle of his left thumb and finger and pokes his right finger through it. He says, "You too old. I take one of them?" He points at Sylvan and me. "I choose the skinny one."

Granny Linda sweeps the money back into one pile. She takes the papers and throws them across the counter. "Pervert. Not a chance, c'mon, girls," she says. She yells back at him that she'll be talking to his father. The man lights a cigarette and sits down at his computer without looking at us at all. We rush back out to the car. Even though I am glad to keep the money Mama earned, I don't know what we are going to do now.

"Go, Granny, go! I love it when you smack 'em down." Sylvan leans forward and kisses her grandmother's cheek. "Did he ask for, you know . . . ."

Granny Linda says, "Yeah, sick psycho. God."

"Where will we go, Granny Linda?" I don't want to think about crazy people because that makes me think about guns.

Some Rivers End on the Day of the Dead

"Relax, Marisol. Go with the flow. We'll go back to Santa
Dorena. We can stand the center one more day while we think."
She rubs her hands together. "Sometimes you have to pay the
piper."

The only pipers I know are sandpipers, so I add this to my
idioms list for the day I see Mrs. Kovacs again. I want to go to
Abuela's, but thinking of Mama and her money, Mrs. Kovacs and
our classroom, my tonsils hurt.

Mrs Kovacs taught us a poem when we read *Of Mice and
Men*, the first weeks of school, and I remember that for George and
Lennie and now for Marisol and Mama, the best laid plans go awry.
I didn't understand *awry* before very well. Now I see that it means
evaporate, disappear, go away like a river ghost or Magwich in the
fog and smoke.

Chapter 9: High Hopes

As gross as it had been, we are anxious to get back to the center to stretch out on the cots and figure out a new plan. Granny downs another beer. I clamp my teeth together to keep from criticizing this drinking driver. We watch the packed traffic on the freeway south, and the many cars heading north. I am sad seeing the signs that say *San Diego* disappearing behind us. Traffic both ways is slow. Is everyone in Los Angeles trying to go to Tijuana? No, I know the rich people have gone the other way, to Malibu. I am counting on Mama and the Beaumans returning soon.

Some Rivers End on the Day of the Dead

I try to read my book in the car. Granny's radio is too
noisy, and the stop-start of traffic bounces my head. If I try to
read, I will have another headache.

Sylvan asks Granny to turn the radio off or to switch to
another station. Granny's laugh wobbles up and down, Ha
HaaAAAaa! And then she says, "Fat chance, sister."

Sylvan shrugs. We play license plate bingo. Sylvan draws
squares on a tablet with different letters across the top and numbers
along the side. The tablet reminds me of my note for Mama, and
my stomach hurts. I would rather sleep and forget, but Sylvan is
my friend, and I will be a friend back. The license plate game is
boring. We can't see too far ahead or behind us. Then the traffic
speeds up where the freeway adds a lane just past downtown.
Zoom, zoom, zoom. . . we are catching more and more letters and
numbers for our game. Sylvan yells, "Bingo!" after a car that looks
like a tank goes by.

"You owe me orange soda and Twinkies at the next store,"
Sylvan brags.

"I don't remember a bet."

"We always bet."

"We never bet." Where did this Sylvan come from?

"I thought you were Mexican, not a user-loser," Sylvan says to me with angry eyes. I don't know what she means. I don't know why she is being mean to me. She's tired. Or she has a headache.

Granny Linda pulls off the freeway to buy a coffee at a gas station. I am glad to see this because of all the beer. When Tomaso gets up on Monday morning, he needs a whole pot of coffee, which we cannot give him in the river camp. We have had some bad Mondays with no coffee for Tomaso. Granny points us to the restrooms and suggests we eat an orange in the car after while she puts the beer bottles into a recycle trash can and gathers up our wrappers and other pop bottles.

Sylvan scrambles over the seat and turns the radio off. "I hope she forgets about Janis. No more noise." She's in a better mood now.

"Do I have to pay the bet?"

"You should. I'll wait." Sylvan is my friend Sylvan again. Maybe she will get her period this week? Mama and I fight most when we both have our periods.

"Granny wouldn't let me have two sodas in one day."

"She drank two beers."

"Don't get started on Granny's beer, Marisol." Sylvan is not mad, but sad. I move over across the seat and wonder about Sylvan's life. She is as much of a secret ghost to me as I am to her. She doesn't even know that.

Granny Linda comes back, but she says, "We're taking the scenic route." She stays on the famous Wilshire Boulevard. Sylvan and I stare at tall buildings, rich cars, rich people, except the homeless in piles of blankets sleeping on the bus benches and weary people standing behind them at the bus stops. We turn at a crowded corner where a sign points to UCLA.

"Please, Granny Linda, drive through UCLA?" I ask. "My papa wanted me to attend a college like that." Traffic slows through Westwood. I watch for a beautiful library like the one at the University of California at San Diego where Papa went to college and said I would also be a student some day.

I prefer Papa's dreams of someday to Mama's promises about apartments and clothes in the someday. The street we are on dead-ends in front of UCLA, where there's a big bear statue and a Pauley Pavilion (is that where they eat, like at East Valley, the eating pavilion?) and a wide plaza. Across the wide plaza up the hill must be UCLA's library because it shines like a diamond in the afternoon sun. My dreams in this moment are not awry.

Then I see a carnival across the athletic field.

"Look at that!" Sylvan says. "I don't even have a costume yet."

"You're too old."

"These kids are older, Granny."

"College hi-jinks," she says as if that is an answer.

But I agree with Granny Linda, and I don't want more irritation from Sylvan so I think my thoughts. Halloween ghosts and witches and even Frankenstein decorate the tents. We heard at

school that the Jens are having a Halloween party.

I don't care about Halloween. I want hats, piñatas, and

sugar skulls, chocolate coffins. The sugar skulls are a special part of

the Day of the Dead. I like the white ones better than the colored

ones or black ones. *Dia de los Muertos*, it sounds scary and full of evil

spirits, but that is American Halloween. In Mexico, this day is

sacred and full of gifts and rituals and special food and special

moments for the family. Last year, we celebrated for our

grandfather and our great-grandparents.

This year, I might have been chosen to ride in the coffin

during the coffin parade, receiving extra candy and congratulations.

Mama and I would have made many *calacas* of Papa, skeletons

enacting his favorite things, writing, reading, playing his guitar. I

was excited about this trip with Sylvan for selfish reasons. I will

have to find a way to celebrate *Dia de los Muertos* wherever I am by

then.

Some Rivers End on the Day of the Dead

Granny Linda follows a winding road across the mountains into one valley and then soon we are driving through the mountains back to Santa Dorena. The smoke hangs heavily, but there are no road blocks. The dustiness reminds me of our street in Tijuana, and I can almost smell *Abuela*'s albondigas soup and mole tamales.

The center's parking lot on Smiley Canyon is nearly empty. Only four cars bake in the sun. Granny parks and says, "Here we are." She's not smiling.

Sylvan and I get out and peek in the front doors. There are only a few kids and two moms and one man at the desks. Everyone else has found a place to be. The air is heavy with smokiness and perspiration and chemical spray for cleaning. The trashcans are overflowing. My nose itches. Sylvan coughs.

"We could stay here one more night, and then maybe we can reach my mom," I tell Sylvan. "She has a friend we could stay with," I lie, thinking of the Beauman's cool, beautiful house and sparkling bathrooms that smell like bleach, Ivory soap, and ocean-scented air freshener.

"Let's call her now. This looks worse than it did yesterday."

When I use Granny Linda's phone, I worry what I will do if Mama is there and I have to fulfill this little lie about inviting my friends to the Beaumans who don't even know there is a me. But I get the same mechanical full-mail box voice. Granny has lain down across the front seat. I hope she's not sick. Or drunk. I fake like I'm searching for my book while I look for more full beer bottles.

"Let's go over to our school," says Sylvan. "Don't check in here yet. There's plenty of room. It can't be as bad as the news said."

"Maybe we can help our teachers."

"Maybe your teachers can help us," Granny Linda adds. She sits up, but I can see she is very tired from the way she is breathing, deep breaths that are supposed to be good for your heart, according to Coach Sneed when we finish a race or shoot free throws. I wish I could hear him yelling at me now, "Breathe, Bozo 12, just breathe."

Some Rivers End on the Day of the Dead

We smell the burned out neighborhood of the school, a rotten, woody, heavy oil smell. Houses lie in ashes, the chimneys standing all alone. Where the school should be is the biggest mess. I don't know what Sylvan saw on the news, but this is not better, it is much worse than I imagined possible.

Firemen are still in their trucks. A large crowd is gathered at the steps of the auditorium. There's no auditorium, just steps. Some of the outer buildings near the gym have their windows and only black on the doors. Mrs. Kovacs' room and the locker room and the quad are black scorched marks, like a giant iron was left on across the whole thing. We sit in the car for a minute, shaking our heads. Granny opens her door, and we follow her.

I can see that some of the people in the crowd are teachers. Three men stand off to the side. Two are comforting the one in the middle. We walk closer.

The man in the middle is Coach Sneed. He has tears running down his face, which is purple like when we run like snails, but the tears are a sad thing to see, and I feel sad with him. The other men are Mr. Moore and the young teacher who was on bus duty when we evacuated. Stan and the pizza-face boy hang around, looking into a trash can near the men teachers.

Sylvan makes a horse snort through her nose.

I point my fingernail into her side. "Don't laugh. This is terrible."

"But Coach Sneed. . . he laughs when we throw up after running."

"He has feelings."

"Right. He's so crying over his burned-up trophies."

"Stop it now, Sylvan," says Granny Linda.

Notices posted on bulletin boards behind some tables flutter and flap in the wind. Teachers are working at the tables, and one of the teachers is Mrs. Kovacs. I am so happy to see her, I want to run and hug her. I wish I had brought *Great Expectations* out of the car to show her how much I love the book she loves too.

"Mrs. Kovacs!" Sylvan yells.

Mrs. Kovacs lifts her gaze from a box she has been sorting through and squints in the ashy sunlight.

"Sylvan, Marisol. I'm happy to see you safe."

"Us too! This is my grandmother, Linda Deford."

The women shake hands. We look at our destroyed school together. Mrs. K sighs, dabs her eyes with her handkerchief, and tucks it back into her purse.

"Most of the kids who have visited were quite amiable about their unexpected holiday," says Mrs. Kovacs.

"How could they like this mess?" I ask.

"Can we help you?" Sylvan grabs the spotlight.

"I'm done here. Can I help you?"

"Mmmm. . . we need a place to stay," Sylvan says with a catch in her throat, and I think about how she's taking drama while I'm taking art.

"Your house burned?"

Some Rivers End on the Day of the Dead

I jump into the conversation before I'm forgotten again, left behind again. "Sylvan's did. And my mom is out of town. The evacuation center is really gross, Mrs. Kovacs."

"Could you post this list for me? The school staff listed who has rooms to help evacuees," Mrs. Kovacs says, and she gets that little cat-canary smile I've seen before and that might mean something good for us.

Sylvan grabs the list and the pencil from me. She pushes the thumbtacks in to hold the list on the big board, and taps the pencil down the names on the list and then fast she scribbles on the list about half-way down.

"Did you sign us up? Who did you choose?" I try to peek over her shoulder.

"Mrs. Kovacs can take two," says Sylvan. "So I signed up for me and Granny. Look, you can stay with Coach Sneed's family. He has room for one boy and one girl to share bedrooms with his kids."

"Sylvan! What are you thinking? Coach Sneed?"

I check the list. Mrs. Kovacs has her name on the list. By her name it says "room for one family."

"Don't you think she would accept me? Aren't we sort of a family?"

"Don't be totally selfish, Marisol, when Mrs. Kovacs is already being like so totally kind. Don't take advantage or make her feel bad."

Granny Linda okays Sylvan's choice.

I sign Sunny Delamar by Coach Sneed's name. My other choices are the cafeteria ladies, and I'm afraid of their food, because they probably make a hash out of everything. The list includes a bunch of people I don't know.

I'd rather stay with someone I know even if I know he doesn't like me or any kids at this school besides the big-time jocks. If I go with Coach Sneed, I know what I'm in for. I can stay out of his way. I wonder who else will come with us.

Mrs. Kovacs has left the table. "My husband will be in for a little shock," she smiles at Granny Linda and Sylvan. "Get your stuff and follow me. My car's right over here. Sylvan and Marisol, could you help me with those boxes? I've so few things that I could save from my classroom. I know they're stinky. It would break my heart to throw every single thing out."

When Sylvan heads off to help with the boxes, Mrs. Kovacs tells me, "I wish you could come along, Marisol. It's good of you to think of Sylvan's grandmother before yourself. This tragedy must be very arduous for her."

That isn't what I was thinking at all, and I don't want to be mad at Mrs. Kovacs too. "I'll be fine. My mama will come back soon," I say, and I almost believe it, when Stan pushes me from behind. He takes the pencil and says, "Amazingly tight." He signs up to go with Coach Sneed. He squints at the list and circles *Sunny*. "Is that you? Is Sunny like *español* for Marisol?" He points at me. "So the S and M team changes a member and becomes the SS!" He chortles and elbows his friend and lifts his arm in a Nazi salute. "*Sieg heil, el Sneedo*," he says.

"That's disgusting."

"Might as well get in practice. We're in for it."

My chin quivers. I feel betrayed and lost and angry and annoyed and defeated.

"Don't cry over spilled milk," says Stan.

There's no milk on the ground, no pop either. Mrs. Kovacs sees my confusion. "It's an idiom, Marisol. It means don't worry about what you can't change. Everything will work out."

"Have you all lost your marble?" I answer in a rude voice. I grab my books from Granny Linda's car and sit down at the table, waiting for Coach Sneed.

Chapter 10: Mountain Goats

Coach Sneed doesn't give Stan a second look, just asks, "Bozo 1 and who else?"

I raise my hand, say "Me."

Coach snorts and says, "Yeah, okay, Bozo 12," and we get into his big truck with a backseat. I am happy that Stan is up front. Stan is yapping about how his parents are stuck in Lake Arrowhead at a B & B (everything with Stan is initials), and Stan guesses they'll pick him up in the next day or two.

Coach Sneed says, "That's a relief." He calls home on his cell and says, "Done here. You okay? Two, one each. Out."

Some Rivers End on the Day of the Dead

We drive north, north, north, way up into the mountains. I have not been this high into the mountains, only the hills. Up here, the burning smell evaporates. The pine trees throw us cool shade and their tingling freshness. Most of the houses are crisscrossed with wood and have angled roofs.

Coach Sneed stops the truck in the driveway of a house built like a hacienda, like my *abuela's*. The roof is tiled with the same kind of adobe tiles, except they are sloping not flat. We can sit on *Abuela's* roof when it's hot, but Coach Sneed's would make a better slide. I will keep this idea to myself. Stan is stupid enough to try it and blame me.

Coach Sneed toots the horn, and his family comes out front. There is a golden dog, jumping and barking, a little girl with dark eyes and purple ribbons in her brown braids. She is wearing a purple leotard and a white tutu and is carrying a fairy-wand filled with glitter. Beside her is the gangly boy I have seen at our school before, the one who helped Stan out of the trash can. Mrs. Sneed is smiling. She is pregnant with a stomach out to here.

"Hello, welcome!" she calls.

The dog sits when Coach Sneed snaps his fingers and says, "Ch ch, Funny Bear" at it, like Cesar on television. He doesn't call his dog Bozo.

Stan mumbles something, but I have been taught to shake hands so I do. The boy gives me a high five instead of a hand shake. The little girl taps Stan and then me with her fairy wand.

"I'm Marisol," I tell Mrs. Sneed, the little girl, and the boy.

"I'm Carmen," she says. "Carmen Garcia-Sneed." She smiles a big smile at her husband. "And our children, Becky and Daryll." She pats her tummy. "And this is Babaloo. This," she pats the smiling dog, "is Funny Bear. Kids, show our visitors where your rooms are. I put clean clothes on your beds. I hope they fit."

"Joe. The school, how bad?" she asks Mr. Sneed.

"Later, Carm. Let's get squared away. March, all of you."

Stan and I follow Becky and Daryll to the upstairs. Becky's room is decorated for a princess in lavender and yellow, even the carpet is purple. She has about one hundred Barbie dolls on shelves, in dollhouses, on the floor.

"Here's your bed. What's your name again?"

"Marisol." I hope Stan forgets Sunny Delamar like he forgets his reading assignments for Mrs. K and his manners with the whole world.

"You smell like a Barbie Q when Daddy burns the chicken."

I am very embarrassed to hear a four-year old tell me this. "Could I shower?"

"I have my own bathroom and it's right here," Becky points to an archway that leads to her bathroom. "It doesn't have a door on it, but it will when I am six." I'm shy about undressing, because of Stan and Daryll so close. Becky shuts the outer bedroom door.

"Don't forget to set the timer."

"Wait, what?"

"My father says we waste water so no more than five minutes in the shower. See the timer? Here, like this." She turns the dial to five.

"Okay," I say because maybe my mother has been letting me waste the Beauman's water and didn't know Americans spend only five minutes in the shower. I get inside the glass enclosure, take off my stinky clothes and roll them up and throw them outside the tub. Then I let the water pound on my dirty skin and dirty hair. I use Becky's baby shampoo, no more tangles, and it smells so wonderful, like Diego and Hermes in the tub, that I cry. I have suds in my hair and suds on my toes, and I think I have new skin when the timer goes off.

"Hurry. If Daddy heard the timer ding, he'll come to shut the water off."

I am so worried about being naked in this house with no door on the bathroom and three men I don't know, if I count Daryll and Stan as men that I rinse too fast and turn off the water and pull a towel around me and I can feel the soap still behind my ears. "Becky, I need an extra towel for my hair."

"I'll go ask Mommy." She skips away. I am clean, I smell clean, my hair smells clean, I am happy.

Mrs. Sneed knocks on the outer bedroom door. "Are you okay?"

"Yes, but I needed one more towel. I used Becky's."

"Good. Come out when you're ready. We'll eat."

I pull on the clothes that Mrs. Sneed has left for me. They are gym clothes from our school and clean underwear from Carmen (I hope), way big, which is better than way small. I hear the shower go on in the other bedroom. It is on for about thirty seconds. Stan doesn't take any chances with the timer.

I run Becky's comb through my hair. When I leave the room, I bump into Stan in the hallway. His hair spikes drip water down his ears. He rubs his ear on his shoulder. His clothes are too big too, which surprises me since he is chubbier than I am.

"Hey M," he says. "Cool house. Lame rules." He turns his head quickly and cups his hand over his mouth like he has a secret to share with his me. "Can you believe he's married to one of you? A Mexican?"

"So what? Have you figured it out yet?

"When I'm leaving?"

"No, that I'm normal? Mexicans are normal."

"Cha--right. You stayin' a whole week? Not me!"

I walk past him. He hurries behind me. We go out to the kitchen together. Mrs. Sneed has put out a pot of chili, crackers, cheddar cheese chunks, cilantro, and glasses of milk. The table is a long pine table. Coach Sneed takes his place, standing at the head of the table, Becky and Daryll and Mrs. Sneed stand behind their chairs so Stan and I choose chairs to stand behind. Coach Sneed says a blessing. It makes me happy to know that a man who appears hard on the outside may have God in his heart.

We eat. Coach Sneed tells about the school and the plans

for going to Viewpoint. Becky pipes in now and then about ballet

class and her new Barbie ballerina doll.

"Listen up," Coach Sneed says. He walks to a white board.

Sneed Family Schedule

5 a.m.	Reveille	
5:15-6:15	Calisthentics (running)	
6:15-6:30	Showers and dress	Make beds
6:30-7:00	Breakfast	
7:03	Brush teeth	
7:05	Leave for school	
4 p.m.	Return from school	(Daryll exempt on practice days)
4-5 p.m.	Chores/Homework	(Daryll exempt on practice days)
5:30 PM	Dinner	
6:30 PM	K-P in kitchen	
7-8 PM	Bible study or free time	(Becky to bed)
8-9 PM	Reading and homework	
10:00 PM	Lights out	

"As you can see, in our house, things run by the clock."

Stan lets out a whimper.

Daryll rolls his eyes. Becky says, "Not for me, not yet. Next

year when I go to kindergarten I have more clock things."

Some Rivers End on the Day of the Dead

"As I was saying before I was so rudely interrupted by Rebecca, here's our schedule."

Stan and I sneak a glance at one another as we read the schedule. Coach Sneed says, "Any questions?"

I ask, "What's reveille?"

"Time to get up."

"Five? Like morning?" Stan's voice wobbles.

"Calesthentics and a run. No slugs around here." He smiles at me for the first time in history and tugs at the whistle around his neck. "No snails either."

"Yes, sir," I say, and I elbow Stan so that he grunts something like "yes" too.

"Where's the time for fun stuff, video games, SportsZone?" Stan asks, which makes me want to hit him again. He shows the Sneeds his iPhone and the screen with a video game on it.

"Television on Saturday and Sunday, not school days. We do Bible study, catechism lessons, from 7-8 p.m. You're welcome to join us." Mrs. Sneed invites. "Since you have your phone, Stan, you can play video games on it from 7-8 p.m."

She shows us into the living room. Before we do anything else, I ask if I could call my mother and then *Abuela's*. I listen to the mechanical voice on the Beauman's voice mail and the ringing, ringing no answer at *Abuela's*.

Stan has gone out front to shoot hoops with Daryll. Becky is whining that she wants to play. The ball thumps against the basket on the garage, and the boys are talking what they call trash talk at school. Stan slips in with the other kids as smooth as one of Daryll's jumpshots, which makes me hope Tomaso calls Granny Linda's phone today. I want my family. How will I fit in here where Becky is the princess, and I'm just me?

Mrs. Sneed walks me out to the backyard where she feeds huge golden fish in a pond shaped liked a kidney bean.

"Are those goldfish?" I ask her.

"Koi."

"Did you train them?" I am amazed that fish come up to break the water for the food she sprinkles. "I love their colors."

"Me too. They're a kind of meditation on beauty for me."

The pond slowly ripples back to a reflecting mirror as the fish dive deeper and swim away. The wind whips through the pine trees. Mrs. Sneed relaxes on a swinging bench and invites me to share. She pulls a blanket across our shoulders. Her garden blooms with gold, orange, red, and white.

"Except for the roses that have their thorns, these marigolds are the only flowers the deer don't eat. I wonder why?" she says.

"Maybe they're sacred? Or maybe they smell too, um, skunky?"

She giggles. "Yes, skunky, that's the exact word."

In the midst of the marigolds, she has begun decorations for *Dia de Los Muertos*, setting out a picture of a handsome, round-faced man on his wedding day and little sugar *angelitos*. Pots and pots of marigolds form a golden robe around the shrine.

Some Rivers End on the Day of the Dead

Melancholy, a word I learned from Mrs. K, drifts in the air though I am glad I will have a chance to share this holiday with someone who understands it, this happy day when I will feel Papa close to me as on no other with a family who understands it is not American Halloween with ghosts and Frankenstein.

"Your father?" I ask about the picture.

"Yes," she answers. "And two of my babies, beautiful twin *angelitos* who came to us too soon to survive and left us between Daryll's birth and Becky's. Will you celebrate *Dia de los Muertos?*"

"Yes. This year, I need *calacas* for my father, my papa." I am not so shy with her. "Can we make *calacas?* I stink at art, and a skeleton will be hard to draw."

"We'll start tomorrow. We won't worry about perfect art, only effort. Sometimes I sound just like Joe, don't I?"

I assume Joe is Coach Sneed, so I nod yes.

"Tell me about your father."

"He loved books and writing and telling stories and playing music and teaching me and my two little brothers, mostly me

because I'm oldest." I stop. My throat hurts with what feels like a
rock in the back where my tonsils are. "My papa was a journalist.
Drug gangs killed him, shot him in front of our house."

Carmen reaches out to me. "It is hard to lose a father. I'm
so sorry. Maybe you'll be with your family by festival time. You'll
see. Let's build something for your father out here." Carmen
touches the cross around her neck. "And you know what else? Our
church does a full celebration of the Latino tradition. It's beautiful.
It brings me comfort." She stops to arrange marigolds on the
angelitos' shrine. "Joe doesn't like to go to Tijuana." She sighs.
"Usually, we travel to Fresno and sometimes we take my mom on
the train trip to Friendship Park at the border to see her cousins.
But this year, Babaloo. . .I shouldn't travel so maybe you could take
the train. Please call me Carmen, *mija.*"

"Carmen-- a beautiful name. You have read my heart." I
force a smile so hard my mouth aches. "I wish Mama and my
family could be together." I don't want her to think I'm ungrateful.
"Thank you for taking us in, both Stan and me."

"Of course. On *El Dia*, we will find a way to celebrate, even if it is a dream of touching hands with them, any family members we can see in our minds."

"A shrine here and touching hands. *Gracias*, Carmen."

"You'd have to get up early for a train trip. By then you'll be used to an early get up." We can hear Coach Sneed correcting the boys on their free throw form.

"I'm not worried about early," I say. "The early bird gets the something."

"Worm."

"Ewww, so gross! that's not what I'd want in the morning."

"It's worse if you are the worm."

We laugh together. Mama and Tomaso will like Carmen. I am learning restraint by showing the good manners *Abuela* wants me to have. And inside, I am laughing at Sylvan, who for no reason I know chose to be a player with me and my life. Wouldn't she be surprised that this home is quite cozy even if belongs to the Sneeds? I never would have assumed this, that something in the language of the Jens is positively, totally amazing, wicked-cool and sick in this strange new world.

Chapter 11: Sneedville

I have been here five days. Each day I call the Beauman's phone and each day I receive the robot voice. As Coach Sneed promised, we stick to a schedule, except one day Carmen took me shopping. She asked me where to go and I said "Goodwill." She laughed like I was joking, so I laughed too. She took me to Kohl's and I found some clothes I need even though I spent more than the twenty dollars I had budgeted. I bought one pair of extra pants (seventy percent off!) and a package of panties. Carmen bought me two t-shirts, a bra (in a size bigger than the one I bought in June) and a pink polka-dotted nightgown because she said girls need girly things. Tomaso, Mama and Papa had not considered girly things at the top of anybody's list of what I need, not until after my

quinceañera.

The Sneeds' house fits me like my new clothes, fresh and new and something I would choose for myself. I like running in the dark up the blacktopped mountain road. Daryll lopes ahead of us, running as easily as my cat Remmie runs down the when the neighbors call their cat—Daryll does two laps to our one-- and Coach Sneed jogs behind us, urging Stan, "faster Bozo 1, faster! Try to catch Bozo 12!" In only five days, my old jeans are loose at the waistline and that's after Carmen has washed them!

When I am running I think all the thoughts I meant to think at night in bed except I fell asleep instead of thinking. I go to bed early, at the same bed time as Becky, 8 p.m., so that I can tell Becky a story before sleep. We start by saying, "Once upon a time there was a girl named. . . ," and she chooses the name. Sometimes she chooses Marisol and sometimes she chooses Becky, but mostly she chooses Barbie. I try to make up a happy story for happy dreams and avoid harsh things about the world. One night she asked me, "Where are your mommy and daddy, Marisol?" I tell her this story:

"Once upon a time a teenaged girl named Auda worked in a hotel. Have you been to a hotel, Becky?"

"Yes! Last summer we went to Sannyago and we stayed by the beach and it was a hotel that looked like a fairy tale. Did Auda work there at that hotel?"

I should know after the first story not to invite questions from Becky. "No, Auda worked in Mexico at the world-famous Rosarita Hotel. She worked at the front desk to check people in and give them their keys."

Becky nods. "I know about keys."

"Auda turned from the desk to answer a phone, and when she looked up, there was a man, waiting. He had big brown eyes, perfect teeth, and black hair. He had a mustache like Zorro!"

"Who's Zorro?"

"A Mexican hero, like Robin Hood. I'll tell you the Zorro story tomorrow, okay? This man wore a red Hawaiian shirt, white shorts, and huarache sandals. Auda wished she was wearing something colorful instead of her tan jacket and tan skirt and white blouse. Auda felt as if her heart had jumped up into her throat." I tickle Becky from her tummy to her neck. "Zingaling! Auda couldn't talk! Her cheeks turned red."

"Tickle me, more!"

"One more, and back to the story."

I tickle, Becky giggles.

"The man was holding a margarita in a wide margarita glass with a fruit stick and an umbrella sticking out, and when he set it on the front desk, he knocked the glass over. He spilled his drink on the blue-patterned tiles of the front desk counter. He apologized and apologized and helped Auda with the towels she brought out to wipe up the spill.

He said, 'My name is Lorenzo Lima.'

She said, 'I am Auda Lira.'

He said, 'I'm sorry to be so much trouble. You'll only have to put up with me for one week since I'm on Spring Break.' Then he stopped to gaze at her bright eyes. 'You are so beautiful,'" he said.

She laughed a little tinkling laugh, a merry laugh, and with that Lorenzo was completely smitten."

"What's *smitten?*'"

"We will look it up together in the dictionary tomorrow. Anyway, they went dancing at the hotel's *cantina* after Auda's work shift. Lorenzo visited Auda's family, her two sisters-- Sylvia and Gloria-- because her mother had died and her father had left."

'No, her mother can't die. How come? Was she old?'

I should have changed that part of the story for Becky's ears. 'She had cancer. Sometimes that happens. But this is Auda's story, okay? When break ended, Lorenzo came to see her every weekend. And when he graduated, Auda quit working at the hotel, and they got married in San Diego where they lived for a few years while Lorenzo learned the newspaper business as a cub reporter."

"A baby bear?"

"I never thought about that. Maybe it means he had a lot to learn like a bear cub does. Back to our story, I was born just north of the border, not far from San Diego." Without warning, tears streak my face because I'm missing my mama and my papa, and I'm afraid I will scare Becky. I pat her hair, and she pats mine.

"That's a good story, Marisol. They're coming for you. Don't cry," she says, as she closes her eyes to sleep. "Ask my daddy. He can fix anything."

I hope Becky is right. I have told her such a small part of the story, and I wonder how she will feel when she finds out that her father can't fix everything even though that's what I thought too. Then I ponder *smitten*. For a long time I assumed it meant drunk, and I guess it does mean that in a good way, love drunk.

I would like to be smitten! Where are the men to smitten me? Smit me? Smite, smit, smitten? Smite me? Daryll ignores me because he's busy with all his serious senior boy things like college applications, chores, and books. Stan makes fun of me for being a dork because I like Becky and go to bed at her bed time. He doesn't treasure like I do that the bed is soft, and the sheets smell like roses, and it's a very long way from the river camp. The room has a Barbie nightlight, and I can use the bathroom in the night if I want to instead of oleander bushes in the dark. Instead of Mama in the sleeping bag next to me, I have the whole bed to myself, and I sleep like a baby. Becky's little snore reminds me of my brothers when they take naps on the couch while *Abuela* or Mama would watch television.

I fall asleep so fast that I not have read any chapters in the new books Carmen gave to me after I finished *Great Expectations*. She says these books are important to my sense of *La Raza* and will help me with my views of the world. She gave me *Barrio Boy* and *The House on Mango Street*. I favor this last one from the picture on the cover. But I know better than to choose based on just the cover because that would be an assumption as bad as Stan's about *Great Expectations*. I promise myself that I will read in the afternoon quiet times.

Some Rivers End on the Day of the Dead

We see the sun come up each morning at the end of our run, the sky painted red and pink. Today when we ran, the pain in my side was barely there. In the beginning, I could only focus on the pain. Today I was thinking about life in the river bed, how it's not right for people to have jobs, but no toilets or beds. I think about Mama and how hard she works and how much she smiles, and I wonder if the Beaumans know yet that she has me, Marisol, here in America and my brothers home at *Abuela's*.

I thought about Papa since I always think about Papa, but this was a memory about books instead of about his bloody head on the road.

It was Papa who taught me "*"No todo lo que brilla es oro." Not everything that is shiny is gold,*" even before the nuns did. Papa used the expression to teach me not to judge a book by its cover. I hear that idiom all the time, Sylvan says it, Mrs. Kovacs says it, the nuns said their version of it until we rolled our eyes at them.

Papa would pull a leather-covered book off the shelf. Each book's side said "Children's Classics." There were two lines of gold and the title of the book above that. Papa would read the title to me and ask me to guess what the story would be about. One was called *Arabian Nights*. I said it was about King Arthur and Queen Guinevere except lots of knights were fighting for the Round Table of Arabia where the men wore long white robes and ate a feast. Papa showed me the pictures of Ali Baba and Scheherazade, and until we read the book, I thought my description of the story was right.

When he pulled the book *Black Beauty* off the shelf, my guess was that it was about an African princess or a black Miss America. I was surprised to find out that Black Beauty is a boy horse. Poppa's favorite joke to tell at family dinners was that I thought *Twenty Thousand Leagues Under the Sea* would have underwater soccer teams with fish like Nemo against sharks and an octopus.

So I try not to judge by the cover or think that shiny things are gold, and now that includes people like Stan, who does not have to remain a stupid, racist clown. He should have some pride, quit letting people call him Road Apple.

I can see another Stan, especially in the morning when he is huffing and puffing up the hill and Coach Sneed and I both cheer Stan to work hard and not quit, and every day Stan goes a little bit faster and his clothes are getting more baggy on him too. Daryll is a strange combination of emo and jock. He practices sports, works out with weights with his father, but he also plays guitar in quiet melodies and reads big books about the U.S. Presidents. I would not have known this from seeing him at school with the football team except that one time that he took Stan out of the trash can and talked to the other boys. Daryll doesn't call Stan Road Apple, and neither do I.

I had also judged Coach Sneed by his cover, which turns out to be half right and half wrong. When we run here at the mountain, he is not screaming. He is encouraging. He calls me Bozo 12, the Trooper, and it makes me proud in the way I was proud when Papa smiled at my reading ribbons from school even if

Some Rivers End on the Day of the Dead

I could not win the citizenship ribbon because of too much giggling with Paloma.

If Stan hears Coach Sneed compliment me instead of him, he calls me "brown nose." I tell him that of course my nose is brown, look at my skin, you idiot. I am proud that my Mexican skin is brown like Carmen's, which is a great change from when I wanted to be as pale white as Mrs. Beauman. I have decided that Mrs. Beauman's color is washed out, like a beach towel after a summer in the sun. Becky and Daryll are not so brown as their mama, more of a *dulce de leche*.

Skin is just another cover, and I hope this is something I can teach Stan and his friends. Taljen, Shojen, Zejen, and I will start a club about skin color as only a cover, and sharing the world as equal brothers and sisters. And we won't let people feel lonely or left out because they are different and we'll campaign against using mean words like *homo* and *gay* and *retard*. Maybe Sylvan can join too if she gets into the right mood.

Some Rivers End on the Day of the Dead

When I think about covers, I also think about our belief in the *calacas* for *Dia de los Muertes*. The skeletons and the masks on that day represent the real part of us that the whole world shares. If you take off people's skin, one skeleton looks just like another. It doesn't matter if you are Mexican brown or American black or American white like Becky and her Barbie dolls or any of the Britannys or even a Korean-Mexican-Indian like Nati.

I would like to teach Stan and all the Stans at East Valley High School and in the white ghetto Santa Dorena about *calacas* and the idea about sameness underneath. Stan would probably call me names some more, or maybe he would learn not to assume things about people and quit judging books by their covers. Sylvan should already know this because her Granny Linda taught me about the ghetto of Santa Dorena.

Stan's parents are delayed, and he is sulking, sitting in a chair in the living room, sneaking his iPhone out of his pocket for video games and texting. Who would text with Stan? Maybe the pizza boy. I will ask Stan that boy's name. I should not use

derogatory skin nicknames. I am as bad as the rest of them.

But I'm not. Daryll lets me play basketball with him because

I don't trash talk or whine. Sometimes I play Barbies with Becky

even when I would rather do other things because then Carmen can

get more rest. Carmen walks with her hand against her aching back.

Becky likes us to act out some of the stories I tell her at

night, which makes it fun to play the Barbie games except I don't

want to play the Auda and Lorenzo story. Carmen's pregnant belly

stretches like a balloon.

We kids shower with the timer on and we read books, and

Daryll and I help Carmen with chores.

On Saturday, Coach Sneed sits in his big recliner all day. He

holds the remote control for the television. He clicks from football

game to football game or watches four at once. Stan and Daryll

think this is fun, but it gives me a headache. The only part of

American football I like is the moment when each college tells

about itself in a commercial. When I see the smart students

working in laboratories and discussing with teachers under trees on the green campuses with the brick buildings, I know I want to go to college. The commercial for UCLA was followed by one for the University of Oregon. I believe I would like either of these universities although UCLA is closer and sounds more like what Papa had in mind for me, the big, famous place right here in Los Angeles.

While the men watch football, Carmen and I are making *calacas* from sheets of black and white construction paper and white chalk. These skeletons are happy skeletons, going on with the things they loved in life. Carmen makes *calacas* with horses to represent her grandparents. They make me think of Joe Gargery in his blacksmith's shop, living as a gentle good man, unlike the other so-called gentlemen Pip met and tried to be. How much I liked this book that I thought I could not read!

I am proving to myself Papa's wisdom that I should not assume, especially if I am assuming negative things about myself. I said that to Carmen and she gave me a big hug.

Some Rivers End on the Day of the Dead

The Day of the Dead is getting closer, I have not talked again to Tomaso, and I am worried that he is worried. Maybe he has already talked to Granny Linda. Why hasn't Sylvan called to tell me?

Tomaso knows enough about crossing the border to understand there could have been a snag. We met a snag, and he had spiky hair and was a disgusting pervert with dirty thoughts about young girls. I have a brain storm, which is different than a brain fart. That snag, that man, is more proof about covers because I thought he would be kind to us, an emo, just because he wore a Bono black shirt. Emo? Psycho is more like it.

The phone rings, and Becky runs to answer it, which is silly for a little girl to think she can conduct the family's business.

"Marisol, it's for you." Becky sets the timer by the phone. Coach Sneed gives people five minutes for the shower and two minutes for the phone, or that's what he gives the children. Carmen doesn't use the phone timer because she likes to talk to her mama on and on all the way in Fresno about the new baby,

Babaloo, and the fires and her guests. Carmen's soft Spanish conversation, like a clear flowing river, brings sudden tears to my eyes each time.

"Hello," I say with my heart beating hard, hoping it is Mama, hoping it is *Abuela*, hoping it is Tomaso.

"It's me," says the high voice.

"Sylvan?"

"Yeah, I have bad news."

I don't need bad news. "Is Mrs. Kovacs sick? Is school delayed?" I know better because Coach Sneed would have turned purple about school being delayed.

"No, worse." Sylvan pauses for drama. She learned to use pauses in her theater class with the emo Jens. "Mrs. Kovacs won't let Granny drink alcohol here. She told her that on day one."

"That's good."

"No, Marisol, it's bad. Granny said no one can tell her if she can drink or not, and she left! On the second day. She said she'd come get me by today when the housing is done. But she

hasn't come back yet, and I don't know where she is."

Like me, I think, now you know. What goes around goes

around, Sylvan.

"But you're okay there?" I ask instead.

"Yeah, but it's like totally boring here. Mrs. Kovacs grades

papers for half an hour, then she stretches and eats a cookie, and

then she plays the same song on the piano—she does this all day!

She calls the song her favorite, real ragtime music, it's lame and all

jangly, and I'd rather put up with Granny's Janis. Isn't ragtime the

grossest name?" Sylvan waits for me to laugh. "Plus, her husband is

about a hundred and wants me to wax the car to earn my keep. So

rude. Mrs. K said you can come here if you want."

I would like to go to Mrs. Kovacs' house because I used to

like her so much, and I wouldn't want to hurt her feelings again

after my lost marble remark, but I enjoy the Sneeds. Sylvan treated

me badly when she pushed me at the school and she will probably

get jealous about Mrs. Kovacs the way she was jealous about

Granny Linda. "You should come over here, Sylvan. Mrs. Sneed is nice."

"With Stan and Coach Sneed? I'd live by the river first, like a Mexican."

I think about hanging up on her for this insult. I try to remember restraint and getting better by one percent. If this is a test for me, I need to get better by ten percent so that I am not furious with Sylvan.

"Maybe those Mexicans can't help it." I use a pause not for drama, but for restraint of my temper. "It's good here. We run every morning. The kids are fun. Stan's okay."

"Marisol, have you gone crazy? I'm your best friend."

"You are."

"Is Road Apple your boyfriend? Wait! I know a secret. It's Coach Sneed's son, right?" She makes kissing noises and then gagging sounds. "Do you make out with him? Granny told me kissing is okay but not to do other stuff until I'm sixteen. Zejen told me some gross stories about what the girls do at parties."

"TMI, Sylvan. Don't be disgusting and stupid. What we do here is run and play basketball."

"Playing ball?" Sylvan laughs a laugh I would expect from the passport man. It isn't a nice girl's laugh. "Then come here. We'll make cookies and cupcakes. That's one good thing--Mrs. Kovacs can good cook."

"No sweets. My jeans aren't tight anymore. You won't believe how skinny I am. And I'm a good runner. Can you believe that? Right here at the Sneeds is actually totally tight."

"Cut the fake talk. Come over to the old school. Mrs. Kovacs is going to a meeting there. The mayor, What's His Name, the Mexican guy, is coming. Some boring ceremony, but we can hang out or whatever. Have Coach Sneed bring you."

"Maybe." Before I commit, I am saved by Coach Sneed's bell with its very loud DING. I also wish Sylvan knew the Mayor is a Mexican-AMERICAN, like me.

"Where are you? In the kitchen?" asks Sylvan.

Some Rivers End on the Day of the Dead

It's hard to explain Coach Sneed's weird rules when I am trying to tell Sylvan this is a fun house to live in. "It's a timer. I have to get off the phone, Sylvan. I'll try to come to the school meeting. If I don't, call me tomorrow or the minute your granny comes back. Say hi to Mrs. Kovacs."

I hang up as Carmen comes in from the kitchen with a basket of laundry. "Good news?"

"My friend with no news," I say. "But could I go to the school meeting with Coach Sneed?"

Carmen opens the front door. "They're gone already. Sorry."

"It was just an idea. I should call my mom again." I call the Beaumans. This time the tape takes a message!

I say, "This message is for Auda. Please have her call Marisol." I provide the Sneeds' phone number. I didn't give away too much information in case the gangs have a phone tap like in the t.v. shows and maybe I will talk to my mama today! A rush of energy pours from my heart throughout my body and I can't stay

still. I want to dance! "Let me help with the laundry."

Carmen and I sit on the sofa with the basket between us

and fold the clothes. I don't choose to fold any men's underwear;

it's too creepy and personal. Why would Sylvan think Stan or Daryll

would be my boyfriend? I'm not the boyfriend type, but again,

that's an assumption. Stan's not cute. Daryll, possibly. I will read

more books so that I don't act like Estella, a rude, selfish girl Pip

loved. I don't think Estella was ever smitten either; she only wanted

to break hearts.

The rest of this day goes by like the others with reading and

Becky's high voice talking to Funny Bear, to her dolls, to her

mother, to me. I sit by the shrine to Carmen's father and the

angelitos and grandparents. I remember Papa and how close the days

are to *Dia de Los Muertes.* I feel anxious and bugsy (like ants in my

pants?), waiting for the phone to ring, for Mama to call me.

I decide to draw a picture of Papa with Becky's crayons. I

put the picture up on the side of the grotto and two of the *calacas* that are finished. I place my book *Great Expectations* below my

crayon portrait because I am sure Papa knew this book and would

be proud that I have read it and that I am working to be a person

who accepts her heritage, not like Pip when he became a snob and

not like Estella, who thought only money was important. Papa

believed, like Mrs. K and Carmen and maybe even Coach Sneed, in

Marisol's Great Expectations.

Carmen comes outside to feed the koi. She asks me, "Did

Becky draw that picture of your father for you?"

Oh, I am so embarrassed. "No, Carmen. I drew it. I have

been told I am all thumbs in art."

She laughs, and to me her laughter is as sweet as mole sauce.

It fills an empty part of me, like pouring warm syrup on a waffle

and the syrup drips into the open pockets. Carmen's waffles in the

morning make the house drift in the smell of a bakery anywhere,

U.S.A. or Mexico.

Now, at the other end of the garden, Carmen cuts roses in

red and yellow and ivory. I scatter rose petals with their calming, sweet smell on my Papa's shrine. Carmen says dinner will be a little late, after the school meeting.

I fall asleep in the hammock and dream of horses and *calacas*. One *calaca* is Sylvan dancing with *calaca* Stan, and the *calaca* that is me is laughing because Sylan is so tall and skinny and Stan is shorter, and they both have such weird hair. They wear matching green polyester shirts with their jeans. The dream also lets me see myself dancing alone while red and orange fireworks go off around me in bursts of flowers and smiling cats. The disco ball is twirling, flinging sparkling light. I'm wearing my Mondrian mini-dress with the short, short skirt and the fringe swinging, my dangling earrings with three hoops, and my cool boots. My *calaca* is a wild, free, sexy James Bond girl.

The dream scenes jumble as I open my eyes. Shade has moved across the yard during my nap. Goosebumps make ridges on my arms. Carmen has placed the little blanket near me, not over me, and I pull it up to my shoulders.

Some Rivers End on the Day of the Dead

I am warm and content. The phone begins ringing and ringing. I hear Carmen in the bedroom with Becky. To be helpful, I tumble out of the hammock and answer the phone for them, and then the phone call is not for them at all. It's not a wrong number or a robo-call for the election. The phone call is for me.

Chapter 12: Breaking News

Sylvan is more excited and talking faster than usual,

and I don't set the timer for my phone call.

"Turn on the television."

"It's not t.v. time here.'

"It should be, I'm not kidding, get the t.v. on." Sylvan

sounds breathless, as if she has run the mountain with us.

"I need permission."

"Marisol, cut the crap. I'm here with Mr. Kovacs because I

had a feeling you wouldn't get to the school, and Granny called and

said turn on the news. I knocked over the Scrabble board I jumped

up so fast, and Mr. Kovacs was going to yell until he saw what was
on television. You're on t.v. so would you just it turn?"

"Me? Wait, what? What are you talking about?"

"You. Television. Turn it on. Duh, Marisol."

"Hold on."

I find the remote and click it. On the news channel, there is
a box in the corner that says "Breaking news, Missing local girl."

The picture is my school picture on my i.d. card.

"They think I'm missing?"

"Shh, shhh, shh," says Sylvan.

"Sylvan, hang on a minute."

The television camera puts the box on the full screen. A
Hispanic man with wavy hair and a crisp suit, who must be a
reporter, is standing on the blackened part of our school. My
handsome papa was offered a position with Telemundo. He
refused the job. He said t.v. news doesn't allow the whole story, and
he didn't want to be another pretty boy talking head.

Some Rivers End on the Day of the Dead

The reporter is holding my backpack and my i.d. card. A red kerchief is tied around the backpack straps. A red kerchief, the money kerchief. My backpack had no kerchief when I left it. Whoever took my backpack took our money?

"Oh my God, they think I'm dead." All this time I have been playing a game with Sylvan and Granny Linda, acting as if we are in a big adventure in a book, driving place to place and eating treats and then I was being mad at Sylvan for choosing Mrs. Kovacs and then I was smitten with the idea of being one of the Sneed children.

All this time I was playing at living a different lie, and now my mother will think I am dead, and I am ashamed to have been a stupid girl when I thought I was getting to be a more grown up person. My original thinking is a problem when I assume my plans are so smart.

The reporter says these items were found in a trash can. The custodian called 911 when he saw the student i.d.

The reporter presses the ear piece tighter into his ear, and he holds up one finger.

"This just in," the reporter says. "I have Marisol's uncle on the phone."

The camera zooms in to my picture as Tomaso's voice comes out of the television. "This is Marisol's uncle." My stomach tightens when I hear Tomaso's voice. "There was confusion during the fires. Marisol called us. But she never arrived. Please help us find Marisol."

"Thank you, Mr. Lima." The camera blinks a minute, and then a new shot shows a news truck and another reporter in front of the Beauman house. A slim blonde woman takes off her sun glasses and knocks on the Beauman's front door. Mrs. Beauman answers, and a woman peeks out from behind her, holding Andy. It is my mama. She is right there, and I touch my fingers to the television screen at the Sneeds' house. Mama is very near and very far away. My tears fall hot and fast..

Some Rivers End on the Day of the Dead

The reporter asks in a rushed, clipped voice if Mrs. Lira de Lima could answer a few questions, and Mrs. Beauman's eyebrows go up. She says, "Auda?" and my mother comes forward, handing Andy off to his own mother.

Andy reaches back for his nanny and begins crying in a loud wailing sob, and I am proud that my mama has such a good way with babies that Andy would want her and not his own mother. But now I feel like I am Andy, and I snuffle back the urge to wail for my mother too. The Sneeds' phone drops with a clatter onto the shelf.

Mama speaks in Spanish, "*Mi hija ¿dónde estás?*"

The number for the police department appears on the bottom of the screen and there's also another number with the international area code so it must be the number of the Tijuana police department.

"One more question, Mrs. De Lima," the reporter says, but Mrs. Beauman tells her that is all they have time for because they have many things to take care of to find me.

Some Rivers End on the Day of the Dead

The camera zooms out to a panoramic shot of our ruined school taken from a helicopter. The football team surrounds Coach Sneed. They have their heads bowed. The helicopter lands on the field. A reporter runs across the black top. Mr. Moore comes into focus on the auditorium stairs, where he holds the housing sign-up list. Stan is jumping up and down behind them, waving his arms at the world and pointing to his chest, looking like a jerk.

Mr. Moore tells about the lists and the teachers, but there is no record of Marisol DeLira on any of the lists, not the one at school, not the one at the evacuation center. Stan is still waving his arms in the background until the camera closes focus on Mr. Moore. I assumed using Sunny Delamar was such a good plan. *Muy estúpido.* Where is Mrs. Kovacs? She knows Sunny. So does Stan. Would the reporter please pay attention?

I pick up the Sneeds' phone again. "Sylvan? Are you still there? Remember the note we gave the police?"

Some Rivers End on the Day of the Dead

"God, Marisol. You almost took out like half my eardrum. Probably, the note blew away. Maybe the cop lost it. Who knows?"

"I called the Beaumans yesterday and left a message finally. All they have to do is listen to the answering machine."

"Morons. Maybe they erased all the messages and never listened to them? Call them back. I'll hang up."

"Wait. Okay. I'll call again and then I'll call you." But when I call, the Beauman's the phone is busy, and I hang up right away. I think about running up and over the mountain to the Beauman's house. I think about hitchhiking to Tijuana with my mother where we will join Tomaso and *Abuela* and celebrate *Dia de los Muertes* for Papa.

I am ashamed that I have made my mother worry that I am gone too, that I am dead too, that she has no one left except the boys who are so far away across the border, and that I would get myself into such a mess. I think about what to tell everyone about my real life in the river, my secret life that will no longer be a secret, and all the time without Mama, and what if my mother loses her job, and what if gangster people are out there to find us and hurt us and now the U.S. news has made us breaking news instead of regular people with regular problems and then I don't know what I am thinking at all.

Carmen comes in from the bedroom. She stares at the television, which is telling my story again and the man is replaying the interview with my uncle and then the one with the Beaumans and my mother.

"I don't know how to tell you about this," I say to Carmen.

Carmen says I should begin at the beginning.

I am afraid, but Carmen has been my friend. I try to make a long story short. I tell her about my Papa and his investigations, the fear we have of being found by the wrong people, the way my mother worked for the Beaumans and how she left with them, and how I should have found Tomaso or he should have found me but it all got mixed up. I tell her about my name on the list as Sunny Delamar.

Some Rivers End on the Day of the Dead

"Marisol, what a story. But now you'll be safe? We better call the police. And your mama."

"I hope we can stay safe. I don't know anything anymore. I thought I was a smart girl."

Before Carmen makes the calls, the Sneed phone rings. Carmen answers, and it is Mrs. Beauman, who broke through her call waiting as I hung up when I assumed I could not reach her. Mrs. Beauman knows a trick called star69, which would make Stan and Sylvan and Zejen use the dirty-talk laugh, but it works to call a phone number in reverse and they have found me!

I need to talk to Mama right away, just a hello, but Carmen says Mama ran to the car when Mrs. Beauman told her I am safe. They will bring her to me at the Sneeds. Carmen says we can decide what to do once we are reunited.

Reunited! I am imagining the scene already with Mama and Tomaso and *Abuela* and my brothers. How soon will Mama be here?

"Better pack, Marisol," says Carmen. We go into Becky's room and put together my things. Carmen provides a suitcase. I have much more stuff to fill it with, and Becky hands me a Barbie dressed in a business suit and her Ken doll. She has colored Ken's hair with a permanent marker so that the hair is black.

"Here are Auda and Lorenzo dolls because that's my favorite story ever, Marisol."

I begin to cry and hold them to my heart. "*Gracias*, Becky."

"Maybe the new baby will be a sister," Becky says with a serious frown. "I want to keep you as a sister, Marisol." She sits in my lap and hugs me.

"I'll always be your big sister. And now you will be the baby's big sister. You know how to make up stories for her. Or it could be a him.

"No, no more boys!"

"You can tell about Marisol's mama and papa and about the girl who came from the fire to live with you a while." I kiss the top of her head. "Who would have thought a disaster could have a happy ending like this?"

And I think of Papa and wonder where the happy ending is for that story? I have read enough books to know now that some stories have endings that are bittersweet. Bittersweet is better than tragic.

Carmen is wiping her eyes with the edge of Joe's giant sweatshirt that she's wearing. "You are a good everything, Marisol. Don't forget your new books."

This reminds me that my copy of *Great Expectations* is outside on Papa's shrine. I would like to leave it in his honor, but Carmen urges me to pack it. "Come choose another book for your Papa." she says, "It will keep us busy while we wait."

Carmen's books are piled all around the room she is decorating for Babaloo. I look and look and decide on a copy of *The Soloist* by Steve Lopez. The cover says he is a journalist for the *Los Angeles Times*, and I go to the backyard and I place it carefully on Papa's shrine.

Some Rivers End on the Day of the Dead

I see now how it is to be alone versus how it is to be connected to the world, and that maybe my father was working too hard to change the world all by himself and it cost him his life. Would he be with me if he could have been more of a team player, and would I never have made this journey if I could be more of a team player with Sylvan and Granny Linda and Mrs. Kovacs?

But my journey has been a good one even when it was bad. I have learned things. Even when I am noticed for original thinking, I must try to also include others. I can't float down the river, going this way and that way. I have to steer in a chosen direction.

I have been smitten, smitten with pride which has made me into a glutton for punishment. I have been punished enough, don't you think so, Papa? I raise my prayers to the clear blue sky. I should call Sylvan back.

I will tell Sylvan my story from the beginning just as I told Carmen. Maybe she will think more about the hardships of the Mexicans by the river.

Or not.

Chapter 13: It's Complicated

I thought it would be easy to leave the Sneeds. Nothing important is ever easy as everyone wise has told me, so that leaves out Tomaso. . . Papa and Coach Sneed and Mrs. Kovacs and Granny Linda, I put them on the wise list along with Carmen and Mama, maybe Daryll.

My things are packed into the suitcase, and I stand at the end of the driveway listening for cars. Carmen stays inside in case the phone rings for something important. Becky and Funny Bear run in circles, chasing between inside and out. Then all at once, cars begin arriving, and the Sneeds' house turns as busy as a bus station in Tijuana at rush hour. This is who came: Mr. and Mrs. Kovacs in one car. Granny Linda with Sylvan in the pinkmobile; Coach Sneed and Mr. Moore with Stan and Daryll, the Beaumans, including Andy and Mama!

Oh my Mama! Behind them are news vans and reporters, piling out with equipment of all kinds.

Before I have a chance to snuggle with Mama and explain all the things I have seen and done, the mobs of reporters push and shove to interview everyone in the house. The only one interested in speaking to them is Stan, and he can't talk to them without his parents' permission. This makes me laugh at the irony. I almost feel sorry for Stan.

There are so many people that I can't hear all of what everyone wants to say to me. I put my arms around Mama. She trembles and has to sit down. She says "*Es un milagro*," it's a miracle, over and over.

The Sneeds let all the reporters camp outside if that's what they want to do. Coach Sneed and Mr. Moore talk to them at first to tell them there is no danger and no story and they should all go home but they stay and stay. Stan told Coach Sneed the whole story and hasn't shut up about it yet. Mrs. Kovacs corroborated the facts.

Carmen steams tamales, both sweet and savory. We are all starving, burning our fingers as we untie the corn husks. Mostly, we are tired, tired, tired.

Andy fusses. Mrs. Beauman wants to give him to Mama, I can tell, but Mama makes an excuse and goes into the kitchen with Carmen. Mrs. Beauman follows, and seeing that Carmen is pregnant, she asks her if she will have a nanny for the baby and does she know anyone who could replace Auda if Auda decides to stay in Baja with her family.

She says this without acting too snobby, and Carmen tells her she will ask around for her, but that she Carmen does not use a nanny. Mrs. Beauman tries to make a joke about balancing her important job as a lawyer and being a mom. Carmen smiles and says when her children are grown up to junior high age, she will go back to her work as a community organizer. Mrs. Beauman says, "That's nice."

Granny Linda and Sylvan join us in the kitchen. Carmen opens the door to the courtyard and the crowd moves in that direction. That's when Mama sees the shrines to Carmen's family and her *angelitos* and my shrine to Papa. Until this moment, Mama has been relieved and happy. Now she collapses to her knees in front of Papa's shrine, and I kneel, leaning against her.

"Marisol, *hermoso*, beautiful."

"*Gracias, mi madre. Te adore Papa*," and I miss him.

"*Manana, El Día de los Muertos comienza pronto.*"

"*Si.*"

Carmen asks us if we can get home in time.

Mama shakes her head no.

Mr. and Mrs. Kovacs have been quiet, not like Mrs. Kovacs at school. Mrs. Kovacs sees *The Soloist* on Papa's shrine, and I explain to her that I have packed up all my others and that I have finished *Great Expectations*.

Some Rivers End on the Day of the Dead

She covers her mouth with her hand to show surprise and pride at the same time. Then she asks about *Dia de los Muertes*. Her husband is nodding his head as if he understands all this, but I think he acts more like Herbert's Aged Parent (*mucho loco*) in *Great Expectations*.

Mrs. Kovacs tells us that school will re-open next week and that it makes her feel like cheering. She pretends to wave pompons like the Brittanys. She pulls her husband away from the beer cooler and trades his Bud Light for a Pepsi.

"A toast to Marisol and Sunny," she says.

We raise our sodas high.

Sylvan and Granny Linda come out of the house eating pineapple sticks, juice running down their arms. Mrs. Kovacs talks to Granny Linda and Carmen while Sylvan laughs at my drawing of Papa. "You're all thumbs in art," she says. I laugh too even though I don't think she should mock my drawing. I wouldn't say such a mean thing to her.

"We have a plan," says Granny Linda.

That's just wonderful since our last three plans did not work out very well for my family and not so well for Granny Linda or Sylvan either.

"If people are looking for you, the best thing to do is to hide in plain sight," suggests Granny Linda.

"You want me to talk to the reporters?"

"No. Someone will tell them we are going to Carmen's in Fresno for *Dia de los Muertos*. Then we'll go to your *Abuela's*. You won't need the papers from my 'friend' downtown because you are with your mother. You can enjoy the holiday with your family, and we can go along with you as cover." Granny Linda makes it sound like we are working for the FBI.

I translate all this for my mother, who is so overcome with emotion that her English is all thumbs right now. Mama thinks that with all the masks and music, prayers and songs, feast and fiestas going on, it is a perfect time to lose ourselves among the people. She says besides, even gangsters stop being bad boys during the holiday. I hope she is not assuming this last just because she wants very much to be at home for Papa's *Dia* ceremony. She calls *Abuela*, who after what seems like a hundred rings, answers the phone and they carry on a long conversation with lots of crying.

I listen in, and I don't set the timer. Coach Sneed paces in front of the window and taps his watch. Is he worried his rules are being broken?

Mama says *Abuela* will make room for Granny Linda and Sylvan, and maybe Tomaso will do some surveillance and meet us in front of the cantina. We will go in Granny Linda's car. I ask the Kovacs if they would like to come, but Mrs. Kovacs says she must help her daughter and her grandchildren with Halloween. I would like to share this holiday with Mrs. Kovacs much more than with Granny Linda. I understand wanting to be with her own family though. Granny Linda and Sylvan have no family except mine even if I have to forget that Sylvan purposely rejected me as family before. I smile that I am learning and growing up to let bygones begones, imagining the next one percent I have moved forward.

Some Rivers End on the Day of the Dead

The plan is made. Coach Sneed and Mr. Moore step out on the porch and bright lights hit their faces as cameras turn on them and the reporters are throbbing around like a mosh pit on MTV and shouting questions. Coach Sneed blows his whistle for quiet, which works. I nudge Sylvan, and we get the giggles. Coach Sneed doesn't even need to make the zip your lip motion.

He tells the reporters that he will read a statement and then they are to leave. He is very strong with words and the reporters settle down like our gym class when Coach Sneed turns purple. He reads a short statement that says the juvenile in question is now safely returned to her family and that it was a mix up about names at the evacuation center. He tells the reporters that his pregnant wife—he emphasizes *pregnant*-- his own children, and the others will be going out of town. He says again, "There is no story."

Officer Hardesty is in the crowd. She comes forward with several other deputies. She repeats to the reporters that they must stay off the Sneeds' private property, and she points to the property line at the end of the long pine fence along the driveway.

Some Rivers End on the Day of the Dead

With much grumbling, the reporters go back to their news
vans. Some start their engines and one stays behind. Coach Sneed
tells Granny Linda that we can cross the mountain road behind his
house and end up on the other side of the valley. He points and
paints a map in the air, emphasizing that she will need to drive
slowly.

It is time for me to say goodbye to Carmen and Becky and
Coach Sneed. And Daryll. And Stan.

We do a group hug. Mrs. Kovacs has me write down my
Abuela's address, she says "just in case," which is like Mrs. Kovacs
to overprepare and not assume we will be back in school next week
at our new school with our old teachers.

The Beaumans wave Andy's hand "bye bye," and they have
given Mama an envelope with her pay for her overtime during the
evacuation. After their car goes away, Mama peeks inside and gasps
a little gasp and says *"Mucho dinero."*

"Good," I say because Mama deserves every penny, and
we'll need it for the plan that comes after Granny Linda's plan.

Some Rivers End on the Day of the Dead

Mama has not mentioned the missing money from the can. I am afraid to talk about it.

Carmen watches as we pack my things into Granny Linda's old car. She says, "*La familia, muy importanto*, Marisol."

"Thank you, Carmen. For everything. When we get back, I will come to see the new baby and play with Becky."

"And hoops with me?" Daryll asks with a wink. The wink goes straight, zing to my heart and makes my cheeks blush, hot and red. I think maybe I am a different and good kind of truly smitten.

Coach Sneed says, "Good luck, Bozo 12. Don't ever let the turkeys get you down." He gives me a high five, and his face is purple. He's not mad at me. Is he trying not to cry? "You're one heck of a trooper, a champ." He gazes at Daryll, Becky, and Stan. He smiles at Carmen with her hands against her belly, Babaloo.

Mama sits in the back seat with me. Sylvan protests. Granny Linda tells her to straighten up and fly right. I wish we could fly to Tijuana. I cannot wait to hug *Abuela* again.

Some Rivers End on the Day of the Dead

We nap on the long drive. The border crossing is busy, but all goes smoothly with my passport and mama's, Granny Linda's driver's license and Sylvan's birth certificate and her custody paper. Granny and Sylvan chatter like parrots, pointing out the colors, the shops, the small carts with tacos and tamales. The scent of meat, onions, and cilantro perfumes the air. Pastel flags, *the papel picado*, for *Dias de Los Muertos* hang at every intersection. We pass the cantina where we don't see Tomaso outside in the crowd listening to a band, doing surveillance, waiting for us, or drinking.

Granny is trying to park near a taco stand.

"My *abuela* will expect to feed us. We're almost there, Granny Linda."

"I need to wet my whistle," she says.

"I need to feed my face," Sylvan says.

"We need to get to *Abuela's* before dark," I say. Granny speeds up in the traffic. "The turn is right there," I point at the intersection, "so try to move over a lane."

Some Rivers End on the Day of the Dead

The traffic is heavy on *Constitucion* Boulevard before the

expressway to Rosarita, and I am relieved when we turn up the

winding streets to the east. On this side of Tijuana, houses are big,

with gated fences, although the road is made of dirt.

Before living in America, I had not thought about the colors

of our Mexican houses, purple, green, red. Some are white. Few

are left in their original adobe. Low on the hill, houses are stapled

together, made from crates and paper.

"Keep going to the end of this road, Granny!"

My heart is pounding in my chest all the way up to my head.

I am dizzy with longing to see our house, my *abuela*, my brothers,

Tomaso.

Granny is driving slowly to avoid the ruts in the road. I

could walk faster than she is driving.

Abuela's house! A tall fence has been constructed, a fence

of concrete blocks painted pink. The sides of the fence are

connected by a locked gate.

Some Rivers End on the Day of the Dead

Granny Linda nudges the car up to the fence so that the
bumper hits the gate with a clang. She says, "Oh me." The four of
us open car doors and peer through the gate. That's when I see a
call box, like Coach Sneed's walkie-talkie.

I push the button, which I know how to use because Papa
took me on interviews before he was investigating the dangerous
drug people and interviewing regular people in the city. We talked
to the mayor of Tijuana. The mayor had a call box like this.

"Hola! Abuela! Tomaso!"

The call box sends back an electric crackle. Behind the
crackle I hear Tomaso's voice.

"It's Marisol. *M' aquí con los amigos et Mama! Abuela, prisa!"*

The door opens, and Tomaso arrives with a key for the lock
and a smile that is unlocked except his eyes are not shining.

Papa, I say to myself, I am home again, home for your Day
of the Dead, home where I belong. Tomorrow we will honor you.
If I were in Mrs. K's class I could teach the whole class the joy of
Day of the Dead. Here I will teach only Sylvan and Granny. *Abuela*

is used to our switching between Spanish and English, which I will do for talking to my guests. Will my brothers still know English?

Tomaso's hands are shaking as he opens the lock to welcome us. He smells of all of the things I have been missing while I waited for Mama's promised someday in America. But his skin sweat drips with the odor of tequila hanging over the good smells. Sylvan and Granny stand to the side until Tomaso reaches out to them. I introduce my friends, using the foreign-sounding name, Linda Deford.

"Welcome! *Mi casa es su casa!*"

"Tomaso! I missed you." He hugs me again so tight that I cannot breathe, and then hugs Mama. He is sweaty and his skin feels greasy. He should have cleaned up for our visitors. "I have so many questions, like how did you. . . .?"

He stops me with a hand up. "First, we welcome our guests before talk about family and business. No bad American manners, Marisol." Tomaso bows and sweeps his arm towards the house.

"Where is *Abuela?* Where are the boys?"

Some Rivers End on the Day of the Dead

"*Tia* Gloria called for help with the fiesta foods, and *Abuela* couldn't sit still waiting." Tomaso leads us down the hallway. "She's catching the last bus from Ensenada. How happy she'll be to see you!" Tomaso says this into his shoulder as he looks back at us.

My guests will use *Abuela's* bedroom. It is the way to express hospitality. I will sleep with Mama again because the boys have taken my old room. I liked Becky's bedroom and my own bed to stretch in. I wonder if I will sleep okay with mama.

Granny and Sylvan go back and forth, bringing in suitcases from the car. I have my suitcase and my books. I put the books on the kitchen table. Mama moves the books to a desk, my papa's desk, in the dark hall way. I embrace the desk and smell my papa's papers and run my fingers over his tablets and books. The encyclopedias are dusty. No one has touched them since I left in August.

By the time we are settled, the bus rattles to a stop and *Abuela* trudges up the street, holding the hands of my brothers, one on each side of her. The boys are so tall now! They fall into

Mama's arms, each one clamoring to be lifted high in the air. *Abuela's* smile is like a candle when she sees us. She is crying with joy.

"Marisol and Auda, *mijas*," she says, "*Mi familia esta completa.*"

"*Los muchachos grandes!* The boys are so big. *Abuela, le he faltadu.* I missed you." I hug her, and now I am taller than she is.

"*Si, si.*" She touches Sylvan's hands and holds them between hers. "*Bienviedos, amiga. Su mama?*"

Sylvan smiles a sweet smile and says, "*Hasta luego.*"

Abuela laughs. "Busy!" She says this like the buzzing of a bee. She steps into the living room where there is the Dia shrine for my grandfather: a pipe and a box of tobacco, striped serapes, marigolds and more marigolds, a plate of covered mole, rice pudding in a bowl, the *pan du muertes*, loaves of the bread of the dead, and what seems like hundreds of votives, She points at more flowers, calla lilies for innocence. "*Sobre su padre*, Marisol."

Sylvan, Mama, and I take the lilies out where Tomaso kneels at my father's shrine. Mama and I join him, but he leaves as we are working through our rosary beads and prayers for my father. I add

prayers for Carmen's *angelitos*. Sylvan excuses herself to go inside.

The television light flickers through the windows. She has followed

Tomaso in. They are watching a ridiculous wrestling match with

superhero costumes. I stay with Mama longer, happy to be by her

side, to feel her love for me, to feel that our family is healing. I

could stay here forever, but Mama touches my hand and points me

to the house.

I leave Mama to show hospitality to my guests.

Abuela tells me that the food is ready. I call everyone in to

eat. *Abuela* has prepared fresh tortillas, lime and lettuce salad, a

seafood soup. Tomaso tells his stories of the fires in Los Angeles

and the work he expects to have in the next months with all the

new construction. He talks and talks and talks, pouring more drinks

of tequila and offering the little glass to Granny Linda too. She

requests beer as well, "Shooters are good," she says. Mama and I

wrinkle our foreheads at this word, shooters.

Sylvan squirms in her chair, ready to do something besides listen to all this talk. "May we be excused, Granny?"

"Don't interrupt adults, Sylvan. Excuse her, Tomaso." She gives Sylvan a stern look. "Young lady, you have enough manners to last for a few days don't you?" She turns to Tomaso, "In Santa Dorena, the housing assignments start next week." She swigs from her beer. "We won't overstay our welcome."

"Nonsense," says Tomaso. "You have much to see here."

"We want to see everything," says Granny.

"Like what?" asks Sylvan.

"Our shopping district, our beaches, the race track, the jai alai palace," brags Tomaso.

"Maybe not the bull ring." Granny Linda frowns, and I understand. I don't like the bull fights either. "Are the streets dangerous for us, you know, Americans?"

"Nonsense," Tomaso repeats. "Danger follows only when people are foolish." Tomaso glances at the front door and rocks back in his chair, the chair that used to be Papa's chair.

Some Rivers End on the Day of the Dead

I look up sharply. Tomaso thinks my Papa was foolish?

"You're here for the fiesta! One more day, our biggest party."

"Do Mexicans go trick or treating? Or to a house of horrors?" Sylvan butts in again. She should be asking about the traditions.

"*Mierda..*" Tomaso shakes his finger at Sylvan "No American Halloween here. Our *Dia de los Muertes* is joyous, not a time for pretending fear."

Granny gives Sylvan a killer stare and attempts a swat as Sylvan gets up, but Sylvan is too fast.

"I'm sorry. Granny complains about my sweet tooth and the way I'm interested in dead stuff."

I don't like the way she says "dead stuff" with no respect.

The stove timer sends Mama to pull warm pastries from the oven. "Come back and sit down, Sylvan. We have something for your sweet tooth. I'll share our traditions of the dead," I say, hoping I can convey a different tone to her.

Some Rivers End on the Day of the Dead

I eat pastries and flan. Sylvan doesn't like the flan, I can tell, but she is polite and eats it anyway. Granny has another beer with Tomaso, pointing their bottles at one another, and then they follow the beer with a shot of tequila each. Tomaso toasts, "*Salud*," and Granny answers "*L'chaim*." I have no idea what she is talking about so it must be a hippie toast.

Besides drinking tequila, what will show Sylvan and Granny how a Mexican family's love bonds us together like a bouquet of marigolds? I will think of something.

After the meal, Tomaso says he has business to conduct. He closes the door to the kitchen where the phone is. "Help clean up the kitchen," he orders me, loud through the door, and I do not like this bossy Tomaso. I would rather show Sylvan the neighborhood. Mama is bathing my brothers. Their giggles echo off the bathroom tiles. She will read them a Zorro story and put them to bed. *Abuela* shows me what I can do, so I hurry through the clean up, washing the dishes and putting the leftovers to the side of the stove with covers on the pots. They will be cooking again, more

mole tamales, more *pan de muertos*. I walk to the back of the house.

Abuela's house is shaped like the letter H. It was going to be

two stories tall, but then Papa was killed before the workers

finished, and now the workers do not want to come here. I love

looking at the sunny courtyard, the chairs, the hammock, the

mounds of orange geraniums in bloom all around with pink

fuchsias dangling out of hanging baskets. We have bougainvillea

and oleanders here too, in more colors than in Santa Dorena. We

have gold, white, pink, and red. The only break in the color is where

Tomaso has cut through the bushes an opening for the electricity

box. The clothesline is empty, waiting for tomorrow's wash. A blue

hummingbird is feeding, and I would like to sleep tonight in the

hammock after a bath. Oh, for a bath with my coconut soap and

hot water, I would do dishes perfectly every day.

I walk across the courtyard to the corner where Papa had

constructed a little grotto waterfall. The water whispers softly over

rocks, falling from one pool to the next. I think of Papa's soft prayers with me before bedtime. Tomaso or Mama has added a figure of Saint Francis de Salle to honor Papa's journalism career, and already, *Abuela* has begun her part of the shrine decorations for *Dia de Los Muertos*, a handsome picture of my father on his wedding day, Papa's newspaper articles, his typewriter. Mama and I will add more books and *calacas*, other things special to Papa. Baskets of marigolds surround the courtyard. I cannot help the tears I feel forming though I know this will bring a happy day, a day I will feel Papa close to me as on no other of the year.

Sylvan stands at the open iron work door of the back bedroom. "Marisol?"

"What?" And I am ashamed of sounding abrupt.

"Do you want to talk?" she says to my sad face. I shake my head. She sits beside me. "Take me exploring! Granny's resting, and your mom and grandmother are so busy. I can't take anymore wrestling superstars."

I whisper, "C'mon. I'll take you." I want to say I also have had a long day and I would like to sit and pray to Saint Francis de la

Salle for my college success and this trip's success and Mrs. K's success and our dream's success, and most of all my father's welcome home in spirit, but Sylvan is my guest, and I must be a good hostess. I decide to take her to see Nati and Paloma.

Sylvan and I walk and walk on the dusty street. There are two hills to go up and down.

We reach Nati's house, which doesn't have a fence or a call box. I have always loved the purple shutters on her pink house.

"God, totally cheap," says Sylvan as we walk up the front walk.

"Mexico, not Santa Dorena," I tell her as I ring the door chimes.

Sylvan sings, "Tacky tacky tacky, tacky, tacky, tacky, tacky, tacky, tacky, CHEAP!"

The same moment she yells CHEAP, Mr. Cho opens the door. He is wearing his normal white short-sleeved shirt, brown necktie, and brown slacks. He doesn't seem to recognize me. He says, "Hola."

Some Rivers End on the Day of the Dead

Nati comes out of the kitchen in a sleeved apron. Her long

black hair is clipped into a pony tail on the left side, like an East

Valley cheerleader. She screeches, "Skinny lady!"

I think she is greeting Sylvan, but she means me.

"Marisol, Paloma *es aqui.* Paloma!" she yells, and Paloma

bounces out of the kitchen, also in an apron, her hands covered in

masa. "Marisol! *Cómo?*" She wipes her hands on her apron. "*Pan de*

muertos. . . ¿Por qué no estás ayudando a tu abuela?"

I feel guilty. I should be helping at home. "*Mi amiga con*

America."

Sylvan is quiet and keeps looking at the street, tugging my

arm and muttering, "We really need to go."

"Wait."

Mr. Cho turns to his daughter and to Paloma. "*¿Se trata de*

Marisol? Eso Marisol? Peligroso. No mas bienvenido."

"Wait, what?" Mr. Cho has always liked me, and now he

says I am a danger? "*Nos vemos mañana.*" I had thought our reunion

would be different. What is wrong with him?

He shuts the door in my face.

Sylvan skips ahead of me and then waits up, saying "What was that all about? What's the deal with the Asian guy? Do you piss them all off or what?"

"Mr. Cho likes me, or he used to." I try to envision tomorrow, the festival, Nati, Paloma, Sylvan. Tomorrow will be exciting and better and sacred. No one will be rude or unfriendly tomorrow. But Sylvan has to behave better, be more open to our ways, our home.

Not too many cars pass through our neighborhood. A shiny black truck slows down to our walking speed, and the driver's window powers down. A teen boy I don't recognize at first calls out "*los limonitas*" and pats his chest. It's only Javier, who was in primary school with me. He's tall now and muscular and his arms are covered with tattoos. He honks the horn.

Sylvan waves at them. "Foxy! Cuter than you know who. . . Daryll."

I blush, which makes me mad. I tell her, "They're insulting us. Breasts as small as lemons. Don't even look at them."

The truck goes around the corner. We continue on our way. We'll stop in to see Paloma's mother. The truck revs and soon the boys are back, keeping pace with us, with the passenger's side nearest us.

The passenger opens the window and powers the seat up from a reclining position. It's Puma, the leader. "*¿Quién eres, chica?*" He can speak some English from his jail time. Why doesn't he?

"*Chale*, chill" I answer, trying to act aloof and fearless by tilting my chin up, which I have seen the Brittanys do at school. Puma's tattoos should tell Sylvan something even if she can't read his lips.

"*¿Ested usted nena? Que tal?* Who are you? What's happening?"

Foolishly, I have already looked right at him as if a teacher has called on me in class. I shake my head, "*Nada. Vamonos.* Go away."

Some Rivers End on the Day of the Dead

Sylvan waves and twirls her hair. She does a little dance step. I scold her, "*Chale.*"

Puma narrows his eyes at me. "Talk. No danger! No marijuana, no *cerveza,* no *enchufar.*" I can't believe he's talking about beer and vulgar words for sex in front of me and my friend. What changed since August? The boys with him hoot and whistle, and the one with rooster hair stands to hump his groin against the truck's window.

"*Cabron,*" I whisper in Sylvan's ear. "A-hole, like Stan." I almost said "like Stan at home," which shows how nervous I am. This is home.

Puma pretends his hand is a gun. He points it at me.

"I know you. Marisol Lima, hot shot, just like your father." He rubs his fingers together. "Like squashing a bug." He brays a burro's laugh.

"Hssssst." I put my finger over my lips. "Do not speak of my father so close to his return tomorrow. Even you know that, Puma."

Some Rivers End on the Day of the Dead

They turn up their music, narco rap, *El Shaka Vega*. They roar away in truck exhaust and tires screeching.

"Let's go, Sylvan." We turn back and jog fast enough to please Coach Sneed. When we get to *Abuela's*, I have the key to open the gate, and then I lock it. I wish a locked gate would make me feel safe, not jailed.

Tonight I will wrap up in a blanket after a bath and sleep in the hammock in the courtyard. Every day my father talked about getting a new scoop. He didn't mean a scoop for *Abuela's* masa. Tomorrow I will give Tomaso the scoop on these rude boys. Tomaso will know what to do to keep ourselves safe, celebrate, and return to the USA after *Dia de los Muertes*. Tomaso is not Papa, even if he stepped into that role now, but he's all we've got.

"Tomorrow, Sylvan, we'll sing in a procession with all of our neighbors, go to the cemetery and eat and eat and eat."

"That's sort of weird," she says.

"Wait until you see the face painting. It's better than Halloween. It's all symbolic."

Some Rivers End on the Day of the Dead

"I feel like the living dead." She pretends to bite my arm.
"The Jens are having their party tomorrow night. Wouldn't it be
great to be there? Don't you wish. . . ?"

I wish a lot of things, but going to a Halloween party is not
one of them. How am I going to help Sylvan understand what The
Day of the Dead means to Mexicans? Or is it hopeless? "We'll
have fun with my girlfriends tomorrow. Mr. Cho won't go to the
festival. It will give us a chance to get together. Paloma's guy will
probably be working. The car plant doesn't care about Mexican
holidays. You'll like these friends as much as we like the Jens. Go
on to bed—remember it's the third bedroom down the hall, where
your Granny went in. Try not to wake up my brothers."

She goes in and comes out of the bedroom, running to the
living room with me following. "Granny's not here."

Tomaso looks up from the wrestling match. His wrestler is
losing, I can tell from his hands in fists. "Linda? Oh yeah. Pictures
in town she said. I thought she'd be back by now." He opens the
door and walks to the gate and gazes over the fence at the street.

Some Rivers End on the Day of the Dead

Sylvan and I rush after him as a black truck whomps up and down past our house. I don't the black truck or the dark, like when Papa died.

Finally, Granny's car eases slowly up the street. She locks it with the key and pats her pants pockets. "I went back because I forgot my camera. I can't believe no one took it." Her breath is beery, and she has assumed that Mexicans are thieves, that people would take her camera. Such rudeness to us. "I'm gonna hit the hay, girls. *Hasta*," she murmurs.

Soon the lights are off, the house is quiet except in the kitchen where *Abuela* is still working, my mama is snoring in the bedroom, and I have had a delicious shower. I listen for anyone in the streets near the house. I am dozing in the hammock with the air smelling of flowers and onions and firecrackers. I don't like the crack-crack-pop of firecrackers and the odor of the gunpowder. I wish for morning and our fiesta.

I have not been sleeping long enough when Sylvan touches my arm.

"The toilet."

"Wait, what?"

"The toilet. And my side of the sheets."

"What are you talking about?"

"My period started. I stopped up the toilet with a tampon."

I don't know whether to laugh or to cry. I am happy for Sylvan, angry about the toilet. I wake up Mama to tell her the good and the bad. Mama gets right up, claps her hands and with no complaint goes into the kitchen to make Sylvan a tea of chamomile and parsley. Sylvan wrinkles her nose, and I whisper, "Don't even think about complaining."

"Mama," I start, "the toilet. . ." when Tomaso comes in yelling, "Agua everywhere. . . .the toilet is flooding the hallway. Go get more towels."

I open the closet with the linens and pull six towels out. All are white and fresh from drying in the breezes on the clothesline. I reach to the highest shelf for our beach towels that we use in the

summer, or we used to, when Papa would take us to the beaches of

Estero or sometimes in San Diego. When I tug the lowest beach

towel, with Tweety Bird on it, the others fall. I sort through them to

hurry them to Tomaso.

In the pile, a cloth diaper is sandwiched. It looks familiar

and out of place both and I tell myself that maybe *Tia* Gloria has

left one of these old-fashioned diapers.

On top of the diaper is a red kerchief, neatly ironed. On my

tip toes, I see three more kerchiefs, blue and yellow. But the red

one? I grab it to inspect later.

I use the towels to mop up the floors. The water has

stopped gushing. Tomaso can't unplug the toilet with the plunger,

and now we have to use the outhouse in the backyard until

November 3 because no plumbers will come to work during the

fiesta season, not even for overtime pay and maybe not at all

because of Papa, who knows?

Some Rivers End on the Day of the Dead

I am so mad at Sylvan and still happy for Sylvan to reach this moment in her life at my house during these sacred days and embarrassed for our family that we have to use the outhouse and to admit that we even have an outhouse. But Granny Linda, who we have awakened though she does not get out of bed, gives Sylvan a thumb's up. She says she's used to a one-holer. I don't know this expression, and I hope it doesn't mean anything like I called Puma's friends and Stan. I hope too that when I take Sylvan with me tomorrow Sylvan's problems, do not dump more dump on me.

Chapter 14: Fiesta

Light pours over the courtyard. I have slept late. Pots

clang in the kitchen, chili sauce spices the air, and *Abuela* is singing a

song from Quetzal, a group she loves. Today is October 31st, the

first of *El Dia de Los Muertos*. I want Sylvan to remember it is not

Mexican Halloween. It is sacred and beautiful, and we will celebrate

as a family.

Our breakfast is little to save room for all of the feasting the

rest of the day. We eat fruit and yesterday's tortillas.

After breakfast and a full panic attack from Sylvan about

tampons and the outhouse, *Abuela* calls us to the bedroom where

she shows us full skirts in vivid colors and tops with lacy edges.

Some Rivers End on the Day of the Dead

Sylvan picks first: the red. I choose blue, and Granny Linda chooses white. The white makes Granny Linda look pale under her tan, a sort of green. Mama is also in white, but the white sets off her gray-black hair and her pearly teeth. My mama looks as beautiful as the day she met Papa, except back then she was skinnier before her three babies.

We copy Mama and *Abuela* as they do their face painting. Sylvan says, "This is brilliant," as she paints white on half her face, black circles around her eyes, on her nose, and triangles of black. *Abuela* shows Sylvan how to cover her mouth and lips with white paint and draw in teeth with black paint across her lips.

"Sweet," Sylvan says.

"I know, right? The uncovered half of your face"—I touch her cheek on the unpainted side—"is your mask. It is only skin that looks like you. The painted part, the skull, we have in common, so the mask is not a mask, but our true human selves."

They look at me the way our class does for Mrs. K, tilting their heads to the side. "That's deep," says Granny Linda.

Some Rivers End on the Day of the Dead

"Awesome," says Sylvan. "I so totally get it."

"Why can you talk like that, and I can't?"

"Because you're you, and I'm me."

Maybe that is fair. I focus on our holiday. I can see myself

giving a report to Mrs. K's class, everyone thinking how smart

Marisol is to know about this beautiful Latino tradition of a day that

Americans treat with such silliness, even the grown ups.

Abuela opens a shopping bag and begins piling sugar skulls

on the dresser to place on Grandfather's shrine. Sylvan and I take

some out to Papa's. "Eat one," I say.

"Epic."

"Yep, sweet, beautiful. Our traditions are amazing. Today,

the dead come home." I stop to try to explain clearly. "This is the

day they are nearest to us. We honor life when we honor death." I

bite off a big part of the skull and swallow the sweetness down.

"We bring out the passion of the person we loved who has gone

on."

Some Rivers End on the Day of the Dead

My brothers run out from their room. Diego, four years old and Hermes, three years old, are practically twins. They race each other to hug me and demand kisses and candy. Diego is taller, he has a buzz cut after a lice outbreak at his pre-school; Hermes has curly hair because *Abuela* says she washed his hair in turpentine and he won't get the lice. Hermes wears a Batman cape, his eyes are black, like mine, and he looks most like Papa. He carries a bag of tiny plastic animals from his farm set. When the boys see Sylvan, they shy away and hide behind my skirt.

She offers them a sugar skull, which they take before they run off laughing. Hermes turns back, his cape whipping around. "Fiesta?"

"Soon," I tell him. "Go to *Abuela's* room." I pat my cheeks and eyes. They gallop down the corridor like the hoofbeats of *cabelleros* on a chase. Mama and *Abuela* pack bags for the day and put the foods into Diego and Hermes's two wagons. The boys will have to walk, but the first part is all downhill.

Some Rivers End on the Day of the Dead

I pack a straw bag too, and throw in the red kerchief and the white diaper. Who knows what may turn up on this day? Sylvan and Granny have walked on ahead, Granny Linda carrying her camera and her big purse.

We line up for the processional to the church at 10 a.m. Today is the official day for the return of the babies' souls, those lost, who are now *angelitos* although adults sometimes come back early, you never know. Tomorrow, November 1st, will be All Soul's Day, the designated celebration for our loved and missing adults. November second is the last day of celebration, singing "This is my home," and other memory songs to all of the souls who have returned, reassuring them they are not forgotten, they are loved, their river will continue to flow.

The bougainvillea bursts with purple and gold along the path to the church. Hundreds of people are walking and singing on their way downhill. Nati and Paloma, where are they? I hoped they would wait for me today at the corner the way they always did to walk to school. Have they abandoned me because of Nati's father?

Some Rivers End on the Day of the Dead

Do they think America has changed me? How would they know when they barely talked to me? And Nati has always been more up on American fads from her cousins who live in San Ysidro. I shake the tears out of my eyes and touch my fingers to my lashes. This is no time to cry.

All faces are painted like ours, all wear festive colors, all carry flowers of gold, red, and white. Petals cover the road and drift in the air as if this were a path for a bride.

At the church, the priest calls out a blessing. He introduces dancers who look as if they could come from Ballet Folklorico, they are so tall and elegant and beautiful. Then I see my friends. Nati and Paloma are dancers. They are dressed in Aztec headdresses and wearing simple linen floor-length tunics, like shrouds. As they shuffle their bare feet, their shelled anklets produce a sound like marachas. The drums begin, a deep, somber drum, but as the flutes join in, the dancers whirl faster, the crowd claps and sings along, and Granny Linda is snapping pictures so fast the camera sounds like a cricket.

Some Rivers End on the Day of the Dead

I point to Nati and Paloma and ask Granny Linda to get
close-ups of my girlfriends even though there is a little part of my
heart that is feeling a pinch, and I know I am jealous. I've been to
America, and they should be jealous of me, but as they dance, I
want to be with them.

After an hour of dancing in the hot sun, the dancers move
off stage, singers come forward, singing requests on behalf of lost
children and also adults. The singers lead us into the cemetery, the
graveyard, where families have set up their picnic for the day
around the gravesite of their lost ones. Neither Nati nor Paloma
returns yet.

Sylvan is trying out the dance steps. "Where can I get one of
those ankle bracelets? Their sound is so wicked."

"We'll ask around."

Orange table cloths drape the graves; yellow flowers, red
flowers, lilies, the scent is unmistakably the Day of the Dead. I
remember when this day was too full of stories, and all I wanted

was more sugar to eat. Today my feet are still and my ears are open. My heart is open, waiting to feel the spirit of my papa.

On our neighbors' grave site the Garcia family honors their parents, using skeletons in bridal clothes. It is an odd sight, and Sylvan asks me if they died on their wedding day.

"No, we choose any happy day."

Sylvan says, "That looks like Miss Havisham in that dumb book Mrs. K and you loved, *Great Whatever.*"

I'm surprised Sylvan is trashing this book, but I laugh and ask Granny Linda to take a picture for my school report. I remember Carmen's shrine and wish I had brought my *calacas* and my crayon drawing of Papa.

Abuela invites us to sit on the orange cloth she and Mama have set out. We break the first of a dozen *pan de muertos*, and the elders stop by to share stories of family. Diego and Hermes run with a pack of boys from shrine to shrine, their mouths speckled blue and red with colored sugar from the candy they crunch in their molars and suck between their front teeth.

Some Rivers End on the Day of the Dead

Tia Gloria has arrived, joining Mama and *Abuela* as they
hum and sing at the grave site. Gloria smiles at me and winks.
"Catch up with you later," she whispers into my ear between
choruses of the song. I stay with them for some time, but I would
rather be at *Abuela's* grotto altar for my father or even the small one
I built at Carmen's. I wonder what the Sneeds are doing and if
Stan's parents came for him. I wonder what Daryll would say if he
saw me in this ceremony today? Would he wink at me? He is emo
enough to understand this, and today I am beautiful in my special
dress and my mask and he would understand what it means, that
underneath, we are all one structure: skeleton, *calaca*.

Since Sylvan gets it, I am confident Daryll would too, if I
ever see him again. Even Stan could understand that much Spanish.

Tomaso moves from family to family, accepting
congratulations on his work in America and adding to the stories of
Papa's life. Sylvan walks with him. She doesn't understand Spanish
and needs to be moving. When Tomaso reaches the bottom of the
hillside, I excuse myself to join her.

Some Rivers End on the Day of the Dead

Fire crackers split the air behind us, and Sylvan nearly jumps into my arms. Puma leaps from behind bushes, landing in front of us, his face painted. His tattoos show through the white paint, and it is as if half his face has a mirage of tears.

"Tomaso! Patron," Puma bows a little.

Patron? Yes, it's only true now, but an odd word for anyone who knows Tomaso.

Puma's friends also dip their heads and murmur, "Patron." The third friend, the same one as yesterday with the rooster hair, sways his hips. He's new around here. Puma introduces him, "Enrique *de* Loreto; *mi amiga*, Marisol."

I fake smile.

"Fiesta! ¿La salsa? senioritas?"

Tomaso smiles, showing the gap in his teeth. His tongue pokes up to polish the fake-gold tooth. "Si, tonight! *La plaza.*" Tomaso whispers into my ear, "Be polite, Marisol."

Some Rivers End on the Day of the Dead

"*Sí, esta noche de cabelleros* ," I say with a fake curtsy, a little

bob of my knees, and what I hope is the kind of haughtiness that

Estella used on Pip so that they will realize I do not mean it.

"*Hasta*!" They jostle one another like little boys. A look

passes between Puma and Tomaso before they swagger off.

"I don't like them, Tomaso." I am about to ask how he

feels being patron, when another group of men approaches for talk

with Tomaso. They are drinking tequila. Sylvan tugs me back to

Abuela's quilt.

"I need a bathroom."

"We could walk home."

"Eww, that outhouse?"

"Sylvan, it's Mexico. You'll live."

"Where's Granny?"

"Taking pictures," I say, picturing beer bottles. "Let's walk

to the cantina. You can use the bathroom there. Okay? Do you

have, you know, extras?"

Some Rivers End on the Day of the Dead

Sylvan nods yes and pats the pocket under her skirt. I wish she wasn't making me feel ashamed of my house and my family and my life. I wish she'd go home with Granny Linda and let me be my Mexican me. She's smart, my friend Sylvan, but she's distracting me too. I want to learn the dance from Nati and Paloma.

"*¿Abuela, va la al cantina, sí?*" I point down the hill.

"*Estare aqui.* We'll be here." She smoothes the orange cloth.

The path to the cantina is crowded, and Sylvan complains about how hot it is, how smelly people are. She adds that she has cramps in a tone that sounds like bragging.

"We'll buy orange soda," I say to please her.

"The thought of that makes me want to puke."

"You're not pregnant, Sylvan. It's your period." I say this as if I didn't panic or act proud when mine first came. She does look miserable with her forehead sweaty. She is walking hunched over. "Mountain Dew? Seven-up?" I offer.

Some Rivers End on the Day of the Dead

The cantina has an outdoor service window. "I'll buy the drinks. Go into the bathroom. It's on the left." Sylvan disappears into the dark coolness. I take our drinks to a picnic table and wait.

I wait and wait. Sylvan doesn't come back. I pick up her drink, go inside and look around. Five men and Granny are seated at the long wooden bar, drinking beer and tequila shots and singing songs. Granny Linda stretches her neck and her tanned legs out, like an exotic bird, a heron, surrounded by preening peacocks. What is that expression about birds of a feather?

I walk to the bathroom without talking to them, but Tomaso raises his glass to me. Granny Linda calls, "*Muy importanto.* Join us -- five minutes."

In the bathroom, I call out, "Sylvan?"

"What?"

"You're taking so long."

"I can't get this in right. It feels funny. And now it's totally ruined."

"Use a pad."

"Disgusting."

I buy a pad from the machine and hand it to her under the stall.

"I hate this. My undies already are hopeless."

She's such a baby. "Throw them out. Nothing will show through your skirt."

"I have to change now. Can we go back to the house?."

"Let me tell *Abuela*. Wait for me at the picnic table. Your drink is here on the shelf by the mirror." I start to leave and add, "Granny's right out there with Tomaso at the bar."

"How long?"

"Five minutes," I say even though I know it will be more like ten by the time I walk that far and convince *Abuela* I need to go home, and assuming Paloma and Nati aren't around because if I diss them by hurrying they'll be insulted even more. "Don't sweat it."

"Fat chance, I'm dying in here."

Some Rivers End on the Day of the Dead

I leave Sylvan in the stall and walk uphill. I'm hot and too tired from waking up in the night. I didn't know that being Sylvan's friend would be so much trouble on our most special day; my Mexican friends understand the traditions.

I reach our family plot. I don't see the little boys. *Abuela* is dozing in the sun, a guitar on her lap, as if she has been singing a lullabye to *Abuelo*, to Papa, and to her own lost babies. I touch *Abuela's* arm, and she opens her eyes slowly.

"Sylvia?"

"No, *Abuela*, Marisol."

"*Sí, sí.*"

"*Estoy llevando a mi amigo a la casa para cambiarla ropa.* I need to take my friend to wash at the house and change her skirt."

"*¿Menstucion?*"

"*Sí.*"

"*El té y una siesta.*" Abuela closes her eyes again to return to her dreams of the lost. Mama is tucked under one arm and Gloria under the other. They are peaceful and content. I am glad Mama has a day to rest.

"*Sí, Abuela de los sueños dulces*, sweet dreams." I pat her hand and Mama's. I am glad to have such kindness in my life. My head spins with scenes from the night and from the morning, and I vow to be a better friend to Sylvan and quit being so selfish and to quit assuming my way is the best way.

I smell them before I see them, Puma and his friends. Nati and Paloma are with them. The girls have changed out of their dancing dresses into bright skirts that match in purple and white. They are still wearing their shell bracelets, and I am anxious to tell them that I want to learn the dance from them.

The boys wear too much cologne and a hair gel that smells like peppermint. I see the teardrops under Puma's eye through the white paint. I try to step around the boys to talk to Nati and Paloma, but Puma blocks my path. His gold wallet chain rattles.

Javier and Enrique grab my elbow. Nati and Paloma giggle and run up the hill to the graveyard. They turn and yell, *"Diverterse!"* They sweep their arms and hands apart as if they are measuring.

The boys laugh. Puma whispers to me, "The boys call her *Escabroso*, Naughty, not Nati. Things changed since you left." I don't like his laugh. I don't believe this new Nati.

The boys push me down the shady path to the cantina. I hear my pulse pounding in my ears, and I drag my feet. The boys simply lift me higher.

"Here she is, Patron," says Puma, pulling out the bench at the booth where Tomaso and Granny Linda have moved, away from the bar. Maybe that's a good thing. Granny Linda leans her cheek against her hand and her eyes don't focus.

"I was coming back. I told you. What are you doing scaring me like this?"

"Quiet, Marisol." It is Tomaso.

Some Rivers End on the Day of the Dead

My heart drops into my toes. Why is my uncle with these gang boys and what do they want with me on Papa's celebration day?

Chapter 15: The Assumption

Sylvan grips her orange soda. She's wearing a different skirt. "We were going home when they offered a ride, and Granny was with them and so I said okay," says Sylvan. "Tomaso said they would find you." She widens her eyes and blows me a kiss. "They're even cuter than I thought they were yesterday. Paloma's mom gave me this skirt." She shows me how she has a sash wrapped to keep the skirt on. "She even had some extra panties, size XXXXL." Sylvan giggles into my ear. "They're as big as curtains."

My heartbeat quits pounding in my ears.

Some Rivers End on the Day of the Dead

Tomaso waits to speak until Puma and his friends go outside. Their shadows frame the doorway. Sylvan hangs back, but Tomaso says, "Give me a moment with, Marisol." Tomaso faces me, legs straddling the wooden bench. The tequila in the bottle on the table is only an inch above the worm on the bottom.

"Couldn't Puma have said that? That you want to talk to me?"

"Exactly what I asked him to say."

"Well, they didn't. They dragged me here. They scared me." I stretch out my leg to show him my foot. The nail on my big toe is bleeding and ragged. "Look what they did. I wanted to have some time with Nati and Paloma, so what's so important, Tomaso?"

"Ousch," says Granny Linda, fishing in Sylvan's glass for some ice. "Here." She offers a wrapped ice chip in a napkin. The ice stings the cut.

"He's a good boy, but a fool." Tomaso drags his hand across his face. "I am a fool too, Marisol."

"Why?" I am thinking of the evacuation center and how he came to Tijuana without me. Mama's missing money. "Is it this?" I pull the red kerchief and the white cloth diaper out of my fiesta bag.

"What is that? A kerchief? Hermes' old diaper?"

"Yes, the kerchief like the one that wasn't in the coffee can. And a diaper from our closet. Hermes wore disposables. You know, Pampers, Huggies on t.v.? All the babies do."

Tomaso's face pales. "So?"

"You took it, Mama's money?"

Tomaso doesn't answer. He takes another drink. He grabs the diaper and mops his sweating face. "Yes, and worse. You will hate me more."

"Impossible. You are a thief." I want to spit on the floor.

"Felipe said he knew pretty girls in San Ysidro. Felipe said he deserved something in exchange for the ride south."

"So you stole the money? You tied the kerchief to my backpack?"

"As a signal, you know, to go with your mother, a way to tell you that I was leaving." He stops. "There's more. It's worse."

"What could be worse than stealing from Mama, taking away our dream, leaving me alone? What will we do when it rains on the river camp? Tomaso, you are my uncle." I wait. I scoot over as my uncle swings his feet back under the table. His clothes smell of cigar smoke and beer and sweat. Tomaso rubs at his face, and the paint smears like those masks with the long melted mouths. I press my lips together as panic rises again. "Papa said I should trust only family and taxes."

Granny Linda pats my hand. "Taxes yes, family no," she says.

"So tell me this thing that could be worse."

"Linda and I have been talking about our lives. She kept listening and I kept speaking, and now, she is right, she insists that I must say this to you." He looks at her. "She said if I didn't tell you, Puma probably would, and then that would be worst of all."

Linda's elbow slips, and her head bonks on the table. She

looks around, saying "What? What?" She puts her head down

again. Her eyes are closed. "Tell her," she murmurs.

"I am listening."

"It's about your father." Tomaso stops for a shot of tequila.

"What else is there to say? I know about my father. Today

and tomorrow and the next one, these are his days to return. I

don't want to hear again what the police and the newspaper told us

about Papa."

"They told us what they thought, what their theory was."

"Theory?" I process this word from science. "You mean

they assumed?"

"Yes, assumed. Lorenzo hated that word, didn't he?" And

Tomaso cries from deep within himself, great gulping sobs. His

Dia paint is almost gone. He lifts his shirt collar to dry his face,

mixing the black and white painted areas into a blob of dripping

gray. He wipes his lips and lifts his shirt's collar like a gag into his mouth, as if he can stop what he needs to say. He tugs the collar

out and breathes deeply, regaining control.

"Everyone assumed Lorenzo's newspaper investigations

resulted in his death. It was easy for the police to say so. The

reporters didn't name a specific cartel, so it was easier for them too.

Most of all, it was easier for me."

Tomaso stops. Puma and the others have come back in,

even Nati and Paloma, but Tomaso shakes his head. Sylvan is with

them.

"Get us more beer and another bottle of tequila and some

beer for yourselves," he tells them. "No *cerveza* for the girls."

Granny Linda lifts one eyelid to look at Sylvan. "You drink

orange soda, right, Missy?" Sylvan sticks out her tongue. Paloma

and Nati twirl their empty beer bottles together high above their

heads. They are mocking me. We all used to be the good girls at

school. Nati kisses Enrique right there in front of everyone.

"Tomaso, are you telling?" Granny Linda falls against him on his other side and puts her arm around his shoulder. "Be brave." She nods at me. "Confession is good for the soul."

He swallows. He holds on to the table and leans way back. He cocks his head as a scatter of noise from Puma and his friends and Sylvan's laughter blows in from the patio. "The man who shot your father, Marisol," he stops again and I want to shake the words out of him, "the man who shot your father was looking for me."

"You? You sell drugs?"

"No, no drugs." He picks up another paper napkin, shreds the edges. "Your father was a good man. He never drank too much. He didn't chase the girls once he met Auda—opposite of me. I got into a bar fight. Over a woman."

"What does that matter? You're always fighting. Everyone knows that."

"In the bar fight, I hit a man with a broken beer bottle— skewp—across the face like this." He mimics a slash from his chin to his ear. "He was a handsome boy from Loreto on a visit. Now

he is not handsome."

He waits for Puma's friend, Enrique from Loreto, who

brings in the beer and the tequila. Did he hear Tomaso? Tomaso

hands the tequila to Granny Linda, who pours a shot for each of

them. Tomaso flips the top of his beer open and swigs long and

hard. "After the fight, I ran. I took the bus to San Diego. But the

man's brother came looking for me. Someone told him to go to the

house where he waited across the street in a car. When your father

went out to check the visitor, the man shot a gun at your papa. He

wanted to scare me, but he had no practice with a gun. He couldn't

see in the dark and his anger." Tomaso rakes his hair with his

fingers. "He killed our Lorenzo. Me. It's me who should be dead."

Tomaso is crying again. I am speechless. All of the days in

the arroyo, Mama working for the Beaumans, Sunny Delamar, the

days with the Sneeds, loneliness, my father in a dark grave and now

one of the dead trying to find his way home. None of this should

have happened. Tomaso urged us go into hiding to cover his lies?

Some Rivers End on the Day of the Dead

He left me to stay alone while fires burned up Santa Dorena?
Because he chose a good time with Felipe instead of the safety of
his niece?

We assumed the people who investigated had told us the
truth. We assumed our own relatives had told us the truth. I
assumed Papa died for his work and his beliefs. All I assumed was a
lie. Papa died for nothing, for a lie, for an assumption.

"Why did you send us to America then? It was stupid. You
were unfair to all of us. To my brothers. To *Abuela*. To Mama. And
me. We hated how we lived there." I shake his shoulder. "I hate
you."

"I was too ashamed, Marisol. I am more ashamed now."

"I hate you."

"Yes."

"No, Marisol, no hate." Granny Linda tries to focus on me,
gives up.

What will Mama decide when she is told this story? If there
is no danger, she will stay in Tijuana. She will find a hotel job. Or

she will stay home with the boys. We will live with *Abuela*.

Everything will be as it was before, except that I have no Papa.

Where will I go to school? How can I not go to American

school and to see Mrs. Kovacs and to see Carmen? What's wrong

with me to be thinking about myself right now?

Sylvan comes back with Puma's group. She is holding

hands with Javier. "They say there's still dancing. Can we go?

Paloma's meeting Alejandro, Nati is with Enrique. Javier needs a

date!"

"You shouldn't." Granny Linda is leaning against Tomaso.

"These guys are cool, they're our friends, Granny.

Tomaso?" she says.

Granny Linda and Tomaso look at one another. Tomaso

shrugs. "Two hours," says Granny.

"Last chance, Marisol," Puma offers. He twirls his gold

chain.

Last chance. I have had many chances, and I have had

many choices. "I'll go with you, Puma. Why would I stay with this *mentiroso y de cerdo*, this pig, this liar, Tomaso?" Even as I say this, I think *No todo lo que brilla es oro,* and I am sure Puma is nothing close to gold, fancy gold chains or not. Who believes this stuff?

As Tomaso stands up, sways, sits down, Puma laughs his burro laugh. I rush out with him anyway. Tomaso could have grabbed me and made me stop, but he was too drunk. He's often too drunk. He's not worthy of being Patron.

I make a decision on the world as I know it, not the world as I assume it to be. Maybe I have to accept that Papa's most important rules are not the only rules. I see that I cannot assume my family can be trusted. I do not know anything about taxes. Coach Sneed has his rules, and Carmen and Becky broke his rules without hurting anyone. Granny Linda breaks traffic and drinking rules without hurting anyone.

Now I will break a rule. I will go with a boy who is supposed to be a gangster and a loud mouth and I will have fun, even if it's only for a few hours.

Some Rivers End on the Day of the Dead

Puma pulls Javier aside, bends his head lower to tell him something. The others all go off together towards the music in the plaza, but Nati and Paloma are twisting around, shaking their heads, telling me no, don't go. I ignore them because they are obviously jealous that gorgeous, dangerous Puma likes me best. Puma leads me to his truck. Before we get in, he moves a cooler from the back seat to the front. He opens a bottle of beer and offers me the first sip.

The beer is cold, and for the first time all day, my throat is not parched. I swallow more. I like the bitter taste. He laughs as I gulp more than half of it, and he opens another bottle. "Save some for me," he says, as he backs out of the cantina's lot. "Where to?"

"Who cares?"

"The beach by the bull ring?"

"Sure."

Puma changes the radio station from sacred music on the radio to his CD of Narco rap. I have my seat belt on, but Puma throws his arm across the seat to pull me closer. I unbuckle the

Some Rivers End on the Day of the Dead

seat belt and scoot over. Why not? I lay my head on his shoulder.

He massages my shoulder with his fingertips and says, "Okay. It's

okay. *Chale.* No more crying. *Dia* is a happy day. All our missing are

near us today."

In the city, the streets are crowded with merry crowds.

Finally, we find a lonely spot to park, looking over where the fierce

ocean waves crash against the cliffs.

Puma says, "Just in time for sunset."

He throws a striped blanket from behind the seat around

his shoulders and takes the cooler with beer bottles rattling in it. I

know he is too old for me, I know I am too young for him, and yet,

I am sure I don't care. I had made a bad assumption about my own

family, and I am not going to worry about assumptions about

Puma. I hope Nati and Paloma and Sylvan are worried and jealous,

but they are probably drunk and dancing and acting naughty and

nasty. I wish I was drunk. I wish I was smitten with Puma instead

of here with him because I want to dare myself to be dangerous

too. Who needs a lying uncle as a patron?

Some Rivers End on the Day of the Dead

The narrow beach is down a short, steep path. The ice plant that lines the path smells of aloe and freshness, of childhood days at the beach. Puma walks in front of me.

The waves roll in to the beach with a wild crashing. Two men sit on blankets south of us, feeding the sea gulls. They turn to one another and lie down. I look away.

"*Es maricón, güey*. I hate those gay men."

"Big deal, Puma."

"They make me sick. Now me, I like a woman like you, even *los limonitas!*"

Puma has put the blanket out and beckons for me to sit back against him. He is drinking again, and I take the beer bottle he offers me. The taste is not so shocking to me now in its bitterness. The taste reminds me of fresh grains and sunshine.

If I sit with him, then what do I do next? Why should I care? He is experienced. He will show me.

I step from the cooling sand to the blanket. I sit down between Puma's legs, and I fit neatly against Puma's hot, muscular hips and strong chest. He rubs my back with two fingers, along the spine, top to bottom, bottom to top. He hums a soft tune. He tells me I am beautiful. I know he is lying, but I don't move or protest. We rock back and forth sideways.

He moves his hand from my shoulder and sneaks a feel under my blouse across my bra. I like it. He lets his fingers crawl under my bra. He stops humming and talking about *limonitas* now, saying "*chichis.*" I feel a strange rush ripple over me with each touch and caress. He unclasps the two hooks of my bra. He twists us, like a smooth wrestler, so that I am on my back. Around us is a weight of coconut smell mixed with his beery breath. He kisses my neck from my collarbone to my ear. He pokes his tongue into my ear, licking and swirling, and the sound is too loud, like an ocean's waves pounding. I like this. I feel grown up and desirable and hot, like a woman, like a James Bond girl, like Angelina Jolie.

This is not the way Sylvan and I practiced kissing against the mirror. Puma's tongue slides in a wet path down from my ear to my mouth and then deeper into my mouth. He feels heavy on top of me, his pants are bulging in the crotch against me, his breathing is hard and huffing, and I feel his hands edging downward from my breast to my stomach and below.

Puma says, "Look at me" because my eyes are squeezed shut. "Marisol," he says and his voice is deep and husky. His lower lip has a tattoo on the inside.

I try to say a word, his name, an idea, but he kisses me harder and deeper on the mouth. I push him back and gasp a breath. "Wait, stop, not so much," I tell him.

"It's okay, Marisol. I won't hurt you."

"Wait."

"No, no waiting, you'll see."

"Just kissing. I like kissing you."

"Like this?"

"Yes, just like that." I kiss him back, opening my mouth more, but I grab his hand to stop its wayward searching.

"You'll like the rest too." He pushes my hand where his zipper is, where his pants are tight. "Other girls like doing it. You will too."

"Not so soon."

"It's always a good time for love, baby."

"Just kissing."

He pushes back against me, grabs my arm tighter. His jaw is clenching. "Who are you? Santa Marisol? Or maybe *chancla*, like those men?"

"Don't be mean."

"*Idiota sangrone*, Marisol. In American, cock tease."

"I'm not. I'm only fourteen, Puma."

"Lucky you! Lucky me!"

"No, like I just said. I'm still a girl."

"And should I pray to you, the virgin? Our Blessed Lady of the Assumption?"

In that word, *assumption*, I hear Papa in the wind and the

waves, close to me, urging me to be the daughter he expects me to

be. I struggle to stand. Puma holds me down.

"I'll scream," I tell him through my teeth.

"Yes, you'll scream," he laughs, his lip tattoo edged with

wetness from our kisses. *"Dame más!* More, more, more! That's

what you girls want from Puma!" He lifts my skirt and tugs on my

panties. "Alejandro says Paloma is hot in bed. She comes to him if

he snaps his fingers."

I do not believe this about Paloma and Alejandro.

Alejandro is not a gangster. He has a job at the automotive plant.

He has plans for marriage. But Paloma is changed. Maybe she has

done the sex.

"Puma, stop. Don't." He pushes his fingers to the

waistband of my panties. He tries to reach lower. I shiver, even

when my mind screams this is wrong. I am too young, he is too

old. I stop his hand by clawing at him. With a catlike move, quick as

Remmie after a mouse, I suck in my stomach to create more room

Some Rivers End on the Day of the Dead

between his hand and my body. I slip free, rolling off the blanket, and I pull his wallet chain. It breaks. Gold should not break. The moment gives me time to slide away.

He swipes his arms out to trip me, but I am fast, and once on my feet, I throw a pile of kelp in his direction. Sand, sand flies, and seaweed blow in the wind.

He gets to his feet, dusting the sand from his face and clothes. He loops his wallet back by the chain. Puma yells after me, "I know about Loreto. I know about Tomaso. He's paying me big money to keep it quiet." He makes a rude gesture with his arm. "Fuck that. I hope they kill him too."

I sprint down the beach to the other couple. They are older, in their thirties, one is bald, one has a love patch beard. I point at Puma's receding form as he jogs back up the hill, tell them he's bothering me. The bald man growls that he'll fight, he hates punks like Puma, but I tell him please take me home.

Some Rivers End on the Day of the Dead

We climb up the now-dark, sandy path to the car, and the ice plant smells different, dry and sour. When we get to the top of the hill, Puma's truck is already gone.

They drive me to *Abuela's*, the love patch man telling me to be more careful about spending time with bad boys. He asks me if they should come in, but I tell them that I will be safe. I want to be alone.

I will decide tomorrow whether to tell Tomaso about Puma. I will decide tomorrow whether to tell Mama and *Abuela*. I am safe at *Abuela's*. All I want is a shower, to get Puma's stink off of me and clean clothes that smell like me not like him. I want to spend time at Papa's shrine.

After a long shower and scrubbing my skin with a rough wash cloth, I wrap myself in Abuela's worn, chenille robe, and run to Hermes' room where he keeps his toy animals. I find his set of burros in their corral. I take them to place next to the books and guitar and *calacas* and pictures. I kneel by Papa's shrine to say my prayers. For most of this sacred day, I felt almost nothing about

Some Rivers End on the Day of the Dead

Papa except when he came to save me from myself. I dedicate this

moment to reaching Papa again.

"Look, Papa. The burros. The asses. I almost allowed Puma

to make an ass of me. And there was nothing slow as molasses

about him." I pray and wait and hope to feel his spirit in me. Papa

already came close to be with me today, and where was I, rolling on

a blanket with a no-good boy, pretending to be some naughty

woman, some fake person like Sunny Delamar, wild and selfish as

the spoiled child I am?

The sun has set. The stars are out. I hear singing in the

streets, "Welcome home, rejoice in memory, forgive all wrongs,"

the song to the returning dead. My feet are cold, my clothes are

clean, and as I kneel, peace flows through me. I am wrapped in

loving arms. Papa floats into my heart, singing "remember" and

"forgive."

There are rivers in us all, Papa said. What does it mean that

there is a river in all of us? I know that some rivers end on the Day of the Dead when the living loved ones ignore traditions and do not bother to remember *los muertos*. I know now that someone in each generation finds a way to change the rules. This one will not change because it is not a rule--it is a tradition. Nothing is as Papa said it would be. Nothing is as I assumed. I do not know what my great expectations once were or what will become of them.

I will use my own intuition to avoid boys like Puma, who believe a woman has one role only. He has no idea and doesn't care what a girl can make of herself. I know strong women. I know what I can be.

What kind of river is in Puma? One that leads into the muck and the swamp where nothing new grows, only the same plants for all the eons of time. The swamp smells bad even though it is covered with the fool's gold of handsome muscles and cheap jewelery.

What kind of river is in Mrs. Beauman? I picture a river frozen solid like that book Papa and I read about sled dogs in the Yukon.

Some Rivers End on the Day of the Dead

What kind of river is Tomaso? Something warm and smooth with no ripples on the surface but shallow spots dangerous for travel.

The river in Sylvan would have rocks and white water and require river rafting that echoes with whoops of joy, everyone screaming and laughing in yellow vests and Sylvan probably falling overboard.

Paloma's river would have bubbles of hot springs like her giggles.

Nati's river would run from Point A to Point B to Point C around a sandbar, like a triangle, and all the wild talk of wild actions would be subtracted and left out like a remainder in long division.

Mrs. K is the Los Angeles river, structured, running its course to the sea. The Mrs. K river refuses to stop for impediments like Stan with his cursing and the Jennifers with their emo tears over everything from messy hair to smoky days to dead dogs in books.

Some Rivers End on the Day of the Dead

Coach Sneed is the same kind of river as Mrs. K except that his river is noisy and looks dangerous even though it is not.

Carmen is a river like my river and Mama's river and *Abuela's*. I have some of that river, a tributary my social studies teacher taught us, my Mexican family. The river is sometimes flooded with emotions and sometimes lonely and always full of material to grow on and build up one's pride. *Abuela* has only lived in this dusty town with brothers and sisters and her children and grandbabies always on the way. She has endured losing a son and a husband. Like *Abuela*, my mama and Carmen have wisdom and kindness and pride and love for Mexico, and they too know loss.

Most of all, the river in me is Papa's river, that continuing burst of energy and rushing from the source onward and if something stops your way, well, you go around it and if someone pollutes you with their hate or tries to use you, you rinse the muck and slime away. If you, the river, must end because someone explodes you like a boulder in a rockslide so that all you know and all you mean flies into the air and crashes into the ground, you

Some Rivers End on the Day of the Dead

trickle on just enough that your daughter can swim on with your thoughts in her thoughts. I will become that river, that truth-seeker, like Papa was, telling the truth and living the truth. In every country there are such rivers where truth is honored.

Papa's river is the river in me, and I didn't know it until this year happened. Both good and bad came from our assumptions. I was trying to do what Mama wanted, to live as a river ghost and wait for our someday. I thought I could be Carmen loving the walls of my kitchen and my home, but in touch with the world of our people. I thought I could do what Papa wanted, to trust in my family always.

This is what I learned from these months and these people: I am Marisol, still growing up. I do not want to be an adult before I finish living as a child. I want the sun, the sea, and the river, *el rio,* that runs free to the truth of the greater sea.

Epilogue, Chapter 16: Letters

Hey Marisol—

I miss you mucho. Isn't my Spanish improving? Guess

what? Granny is going to AA and she says we can come to visit

you over Christmas break if your grandmother and mother say it's

okay. Oh, and guess what else? I'm running for Student Council

next semester because Mrs. K says they need more original

thinking. Coach Sneed still hates me, so big deal. I'm trying out for

the school play with the emo Jens. We work on our parts after

school. The play is called "A Christmas Carol" by that same Great

Regurgitations author, but I kind of like it. I want to be Christmas Future!

Gotta go, write me soon, love ya, mis amiga. Sylvan

Ps—Granny says hi! And hi to Tomaso (do you think those two have a thing going?)

Pps—The Road Apple, Stan, says hi. Gag.

Ppps—Daryll is going out with Shojen. He's pretty nice for a jock; we talk about you sometimes! Wish you were here so he could take you to Winter Formal. I'm not going unless they let us go without dates. Could you see if Javier would come up for that weekend? He could stay with Coach Sneed or Mrs. K, I bet.

Your BFF, Sylvan

Dear Marisol,

How is your new school, dear? Are you reading the books on your book list?

The class is working hard on their projects about the Victorian Era and the customs of Christmas. After all that you

Some Rivers End on the Day of the Dead

have written to me about *Dia de los Muertes* and the report Sylvan

gave to the class including pictures, I will have a new project next

year: Edgar Allan Poe and Washington Irving and the traditions of

the harvest and All Souls Day.

I hope your teachers appreciate your original thinking and

that you will continue to write to me. You are the kind of student a

teacher dreams of having, Marisol. You have kindness and courage

and intelligence. I am so proud to have been your teacher, and I

want to be there on the day you receive your diploma from a

famous university.

Warm regards, Mrs. K

Dear Marisol,

The baby is here! It's a girl! I have named her Solimar, can

you guess why? She has a quizzical look on her face all the time as

if she is asking questions. That reminds me of you, Marisol.

Solimar has a full head of dark black hair, a round face with chubby

cheeks, and little lips like rosebuds. She weighed eight pounds when she was born! Becky doesn't understand why she can't dress Solimar in pretty Barbie outfits instead of in onesies.

Her full name is Solimar Ruth Garcia-Sneed. Do you think that's too big a name for a little girl? I want her to be beautiful and smart and conscious of her Latina heritage. I'm reading to her already the poems of Octavio Paz. She listens with her big eyes blinking and her forehead scrunching up.

All of us are well and talk often about having you and Stan stay with us during the fires. Daryll says he misses the morning runs and the basketball, Becky says she misses you telling her stories in the night, and my husband says he wants Becky to be more like you (that is, he wishes she would be quiet sometimes). I miss having you as a companion and a little sponge who had such eagerness to read and to learn. We had fun making the *calacas*, didn't we? I will put them out every year for *El Dia de los Muertes*. I told my mother about you, and she agrees that you will be a famous woman someday!

Some Rivers End on the Day of the Dead

Write to me soon to tell me if you can be Solimar's
godmother, which could honor us if you accept.

I hear Solimar crying for her feeding again. I am sending
love to you, your mama, and your *abuela*. Joe says to tell you you're
a champ. Becky will add her own note. Carmen

P.S. I love you, from Becky. I tell Solimar stories. I like her name.

Dear Mrs. Lira and Mrs. Sneed,

We hope this card finds you well. Do you have any
recommendations as you suggested you might for a nanny? Andy
has grown so much since you left us. He is crawling now and a
bigger darling. Such a handful! And now I find I'm going to have
another baby. I will really need a new nanny before summer.

Sincerely yours, Cindy Beauman

Some Rivers End on the Day of the Dead

Dear Everyone,

I am fine. School is excellent. Papa's insurance money paid us at last when his name was cleared.

Mama used the extra money from the insurance and the Beaumans to put me into a private school for preparation for the university! The exams were hard, but I scored a high score in English and language which helped balance my lower score in the mathematics. My teachers are quite serious and we don't do fun projects and there aren't any boys at the school to distract us from our studies. I am reading a Russian author, Tolstoy, because it was the longest, hardest book I could find, *War and Peace.* But my literature teacher said I should not discount Gabriel Garcia Marquez and Isabel Allende, so those two will be next. And I appreciate your suggestion of *Don Quixote* for next summer, Mrs. K. Also, I am sorry your copy of *An American Tragedy* got lost. I will buy a new one to send you. I hope's it's okay if I read it first!

Some Rivers End on the Day of the Dead

I am happy to hear all the good news from America, especially about Solimar! I wish that I could be her godmother, but I cannot come to the baptism and that would not be right. I will always be Solimar's special sister as I am Becky's.

I am also very happy to be home in Mexico, despite our many adventures getting here and on *Dia de los Muertes*. I will write each of you an individual message, but I am going to do my homework soon. I like having a computer to work from!

We are studying ancient history, the Egyptians, which I like a lot although I would rather read about the Aztecs and the Mayans. I do not want to assume one culture is more important than another, so I am studying everything the teachers give to me.

Much happened in my time in America, and all of you have helped to change me. My *quinceañera* is in May, only six months away! Becky and Sylvan, would you be on my court of honor with Nati and Paloma? Nati and Paloma don't go to my school, but they are friends with me again, more on that in a minute.

Some Rivers End on the Day of the Dead

Your dresses will be sea green and my dress will be golden-yellow like sunshine. Mama, *Abuela*, and I are going *loco* planning for all the details since we are getting such a late start, and I hope that you will come.

Tomaso and I are practicing a waltz with a dancing teacher, which is very funny if you can picture Tomaso--or me-- waltzing! I finally get to use the gift certificate for my dancing lessons. The dancing teacher is so stern, like Coach Sneed, that I think he will start calling me Bozo 12.

Tomaso is going to AA just like Granny Linda. He is working on making reparations to all of those he hurt, me and Mama, and the family of the young man with the scar from Loreto. Enrique knows that boy, and they went together to pray with his mother. The boy and his brother had left for Ciudad Juarez or El Paso. Now Puma has nothing to hold over Tomaso's head for money or for reputation because these troublesome cats are all out of the bag.

Some Rivers End on the Day of the Dead

Before Tomaso started AA, Mama said she would never speak to him again, but we met with our priest after confession, and he helped Tomaso choose AA. Tomaso even talked to Mr. Cho so that Nati could be friends with me again.

The priest suggested a grief group for me and for Mama.

We have cried a lot. Our group laughs and cries; sometimes, we draw (I am still all thumbs). Sometimes, we journal. All of this has helped us to stop thinking we could run away from grief.

Here is a line from a poem I am writing to read at my *quinceañera:*

Love is like a river, flowing to a greater sea.

Love, Marisol

Acknowledgments

I am grateful for the energy and inspiration of my UCLA
teachers, especially Eve Caram, Steven Wolfson, Van Khanna, and
Cecilia Brainard; the keen-eyed help of my editors, Kathleen
Penrice and Molly Lyons; the laughter and joy of my reading
circle—Eve Caram, Judi Turner, Valerie Garret Miller, and Susan
Ware; my online classmates—Yvette Johnson and Caroline McCoy.

Special thanks to the talented Martha Rodriguez for
copyright permission to use *Calavera A-Go-Go* on the cover of this
book.

My teen readers, Jonathan Penrice, Hiarpi Airapetyan, and
Alik Airapetyan, helped me keep it real.

Sending profound love to my high school friends who have
cheered me on, and to my husband, Patrick, and my children,
Aaron and Alisha, who have watched this process unfold over so
many, many years.

To my parents, here and in the great beyond, Mama, Poppa,
Patti, Gene, and Ronnie, I hope this makes you proud.

Resources:

To learn more about *El Dia de los Muertos*, here are some sources that I found infinitely helpful:

Books:

Lowery, Linda, *The Day of the Dead*, Carolrhoda Books, 2004.

Vanderwood, Paul J., *Juan Soldado*, Duke University Press, 2006.

Films:

The Day of the Dead: A Celebration of Family and Life (documentary)

Web Sites:

http://www.dayofthedead.com

www.inside-mexico.com/featuredead.htm

About the author

Eileen Clemens Granfors lives in Santa Clarita, California, with her husband and two dogs. A former army brat, Eileen is a proud UCLA alum. She joined the UCLA Writers' Extension Program after retiring from thirty-four years of teaching high school English. Her work has been published in the *Cup of Comfort* series, the *Ozarks Mountaineer*, *Bark Magazine Online*, and *WOW (Women on Writing) online*.

She has completed a volume of poetry ("White Sheets"), two novels, and is working on the other books in the Marisol Trilogy, *The Piñata-Maker's Daughter* and *So You, Solimar*. She also is researching life in eighteenth century England and France for a book long-promised to her former students, *A Tale of Two Cities: The Prequel*.

Follow her on authorsden.com, goodreads.com and on her blog, "Word Joy," at www.eileengranfors.blogspot.com. To keep up on the progress of the Marisol trilogy and to learn more about the Day of the Dead traditions, follow Marisol on her blog: www.marisolsomeriversend.blogpot.com

About the artist

Martha Rodriguez calls herself an urban folk artist, whose calling has come after careers in social welfare and education. Attending college during the student movements of the 1970s, the pride and rich history of her Chicano/Mexicano ancestors became an integral part of her life. She is self-taught, influenced by her life as a native Californian, urban dweller and child of 60s pop. She is also drawn to the decade of the 1940s and to the people and culture of New Orleans.

She is a painter, mixed media artist, and installation artist, who creates altars for Day of the Dead and designs icon image jewelry, crossing the lines of all media.

Some of the artists most influential to her have been the Mexican muralists of the early 20th century, as well as the work of Andy Warhol. Raised in the Mexican-American Baptist church, she is fascinated by Catholic religious icons. Her color palette is rich in primary colors, with scarlet red being dominant. She is a Chicana, saying, "My artistic endeavors reflect the duality of growing-up American with roots forever planted in beloved Mexico."

Reading Guide:

1. How does the cover art by Martha Rodriguez draw you into the story along with the title?

2. Which of the people Marisol meets in Santa Dorena has the strongest influence on her? Why do you feel that way?

3. How does Granny Linda break the stereotype of a hippie grandmother? How does that label fit her?

4. What did you learn about *El Dia de los Muertos* from Marisol's explanations and actions? Did this book enhance your understanding of the importance of the holiday in other cultures?

5. Is Sylvan a best friend or a *frenemy*? Does their relationship remind you of any you have had in your life?

6. Marisol is addicted to books. Have you read or will you now read any of the titles she shares during her journey? How do these books impact her actions and thoughts?

7. How does the imagery of the river change as Marisol changes? Do you agree with Lorenzo and Marisol that "there is a river in all of us"?

8. If you wrote a letter to Marisol, what would you ask her and when would you write to her, before or after her *quinceañera*? Why?

9. Were you surprised about Marisol's choice on the beach?

10. What theme stands out most strongly to you in this book?

11. The author plans a trilogy, including a prequel. Would you want to read more about Sylvan, Stan, the Jens, Auda, Carmen? Why?

12. What role does family play in this book? How are families defined differently by the actions of the parents?

13. Compare and contrast the suburban setting of Santa Dorena with the urban settings of Los Angeles and Tijuana.

14. Who would you cast in the role of Marisol in a filmed version of this book? Granny Linda? Carmen? Coach Sneed?

15. The final book of the trilogy, *So You, Solimar*, will focus on Solimar Sneed in her high school years, so sixteen years will pass after this book ends. What direction do you imagine Marisol will go for her career in that book?

16. Marisol struggles with American idioms. Look up the history of one of the idioms to share with your book club or fellow readers. Do you have experiences with explaining idioms to your children or others?

Notes:

Some Rivers End on the Day of the Dead